The House on
Figueroa: Stories

The House on Figueroa: Stories

Dorian Gossy

Hamilton Stone Editions
Maplewood, New Jersey

H\s
Editions

Library of Congress Cataloging-in-Publication Data
Names: Gossy, Dorian, author.
Title: The house on Figueroa / short stories by Dorian Gossy.
Other titles: House on Figueroa (Compilation)
Description: Maplewood, New Jersey : Hamilton Stone Editions, [2023] |
Summary: "The five-story Victorian house on Figueroa in this book of short stories is both a real place and a mythical way station where people must face changing fortunes that complicate even the most ordinary lives. Immigrants struggle to adapt, failure looms at the edges of happy marriages, even the most benign circumstances threaten sanity itself. The defining conflicts in The House on Figueroa are sharply delineated in crisp prose fresh imagery: wind that smells like a chainsaw, a Mexican sweetcake in a jewelry box, a painting with crushed roses broken glass. A dying woman banishes her husband from her sick-bed, a scientist fudges an important experiment. What happens next? How do people survive irrevocable changes? Delve into this collection and find out"-- Provided by publisher.
Identifiers: LCCN 2022028408 | ISBN 9781736500125 (trade paperback)
Subjects: LCGFT: Short stories.
Classification: LCC PS3607.O857 H68 2023 | DDC 813/.6--dc23/eng/20220708
LC record available at https://lccn.loc.gov/2022028408

Hamilton Stone Editions
Maplewood, New Jersey
Hamiltonstone.org

Cover design by Adalberto Ortiz
Interior Design by WSM Technical

For Roger, always

And for

Dad
Bill
Laurie
Trisha
Dan
Elyse
Daniel
Lisa
Paul
Wesley
Billy

And in memory of Betty Gossy

My Lovies

Table of Contents

Part I
Half-Truths

1 Bad

For a long time after Dan's death I met only sympathy. Even the mirthless hall monitor came to the funeral and squeezed my hand. I knew them all, the teachers, school nurses, principals, lunchroom ladies, playground assistants, school psychologists, plus the outside professionals: the psychiatrists, behaviorists, endocrinologists, astrologers, psychics—people who tried to help my son and me. Everything worked for a little while. Dan would settle into himself, and his eyes would focus and deepen with understanding. Oh, at those times I could foresee him a president, a great healing doctor, a sage.

*

I'd always wanted children, but my early circumstances didn't favor it. There was college, and then office work and friends and men and music and nights out, all competing for my attention. Looking back at photos, it seems I was something of a beauty, though I could not see this at the time. Though all three of my sisters also turned out blonde, none of them got the icy starkness that I did, the sort of coloring that looks fake and otherworldly. Though I was a little too thin and angular, there was something about my being so blonde that drew men's eyes to me, as if they'd been looking for a bright open door in the dark. Sometimes I relished the pressure of their gazes, and other times, I wanted to collapse and hide, and occasionally did. I tried black lipstick, or a dark red rinse. When I turned thirty my looks softened, as did the hungry stares. I could ease up on my wariness enough to notice the long-term pleasures of other people's lives, their homes and families and well-plotted futures.

At first, the men I considered for marriage too closely resembled the capricious boys who kept me company in my teens and twenties. There were weeks and months of rapture, followed by a wane in interest. All the breakups were genial, so I enjoyed a widening circle of former lovers morphed into friends. By the time I was thirty-four, there were a dozen new names on my Christmas card list but no one to marry. By thirty-five, I considered adopting a child by myself, or asking a fertilization favor of one of these former lovers, but I drew up short. I was sensible. I knew about the difficulties of raising children. I began to think it might never happen. I prepared myself to be a good friend to many, and to do without a husband and family.

And then I met Nathan, as easily and naturally as if he'd been waiting outside for a long prearranged appointment. He'd even gone to the same large high school I had. I like to think we passed in the halls, sharing oxygen molecules, he a glamorous senior, me a wispy blonde freshman, so thin and small that when the wind blew hard, I'd have to be steadied by nearby friends. We met at an airport right after my thirty-fifth birthday, while waiting for different delayed flights. I was going to visit a sister; he was on a business trip for the software firm for whom he creates marketing schemes. Neither of us made our flights, as we both took the flight vouchers in exchange for our seats on the overbooked planes. We went to dinner in one of the elegant airport hotels instead, and spent the night together in a suite, offering fictional excuses and then the amused truth to our families and co-workers and bosses. When we married eight months later, we held the wedding at this same hotel.

We bought a house together, got a dog from the pound, and found ourselves in complete accord on everything from taste in drape and carpet to how eagerly we wanted to have children. Our bodies obliged, and I became pregnant within two months of our wedding. I felt God smiling on us and on me, and I don't even believe in God. I figured there had to be supernatural help for such abundance, after I'd nearly given up. We had apple trees in our large yard, and that fall they bore as they never did again. I went from house to house in our upstate New York neighborhood, offering the surplus to our new neighbors. Later, these same neighbors confided they thought me possessed then as I went door to door, grinning, my pregnant skin glowing, my wild yellow hair boiling around me in the changeable autumn breezes.

The first miscarriage at eight weeks dismayed Nathan more than me, since I'd read the books. I knew that doctors called mine a "geri-atric" pregnancy, and miscarriages were more common for women my age. The second miscarriage at twelve weeks, just six months later, sent me to bed for longer than it took to truly recover. I was thinking, and that took all my time. I decided I had one more try in me, and told Nathan, who was watching me miserably for what to do next. We con-sulted a deeper tier of specialist doctors, who put me through a series of reproductive regimes, including a barrage of hormones that in-duced a temporary menopause. Each of these schemes made scientific sense to me at the time, though now I only remember the vomiting and the exhaustion, the way animals remember with their bodies.

When I became pregnant again, for the third and last time, I bought a cheap necklace dangling a tiny glass deer figurine and wore it day and night. I never broke it, and that was the idea. As long as I behaved as if I were glass, I would get my baby. And later that year, three weeks earlier than his due date, Dan came screaming into our world, black-haired like Nathan, whole and perfect, one fist full of umbilical cord as if the last instruction he'd been given before his release to us was, *hold on.*

*

Dan's death certificate says asphyxiation by water accident. He was eight years, seven months, and six days old. He wasn't conscious at the time he went below the surface of the water, so his drowning was rel-atively peaceful. I read about this later, taking comfort in the unadorned details. The lungs take on water like a sponge, and without oxygen, brain systems shut down after only minutes. His body must have suffered, but his mind was already down its last dark road.

Back when I breastfed him, sometimes he'd fix his gaze on mine in the widest terror, as though he was seeing something frightening in my face, or something inside his own head from which he could not escape. I'd usually be able to jiggle him back from this brink. But sometimes he bit me hard and began a terrible chorus of screeches and sobs. My companions at the new mother support group could not offer any explanations, moving instead to nipple-biting stories with knowing laughter. Dan's pediatrician said, he'll grow out of it. In some ways Dan's birth and death were the easiest parts of his life. During those times the body's tasks are so simple.

*

Dan's difficulties started early. Even our specialists called them nothing more scientific than difficulties, their source apparently being in a cluster of so many physiological and psychological abnormalities that no one name could be given them, or him. He would smile in my face, or in Nathan's, and then strike out hard, with a tiny fist, at nine months old.

As those early years went by, we stopped having to explain our bruises to family and close friends. In groups of other children, at first he'd imitate them, be docile, follow instructions from teachers and aides, and then he'd kick or bite or hit, without warning, and often he said he didn't remember what he'd done, so suddenly would the impulse to act snake out of its twisted synapse and retreat again. Only later, when other children and adults began to hate him, did Dan grow mean, but I'm still convinced that their hatred made him mean, and gave the edge to his violence by which the world came to know him. He honestly did not know what he was doing when, at fourteen months old, he broke Nathan's nose. It was just the angle of the strike, and the fact that Nathan had broken his nose before, during a wrestling match in high school. You should have seen the cheer in Dan's face at the time, until he saw the blood run from his father's nose and heard Nathan wince and moan.

Yes, we tried antidepressants and antipsychotics and antiepileptics and Ritalin and Xanax and treatment for Tourette's, and other things, including some compounds never used for emotional disturbance before, as part of a clinical trial. All of it sluiced through his system, useless. When he was six, Dan's case was written up in a psychiatric journal for his unusual resistance to medication. The only thing that had any effect on him was Halcion, which put him to sleep. We kept some on hand for severe situations, as when Dan would cry himself into a frenzy after a particularly bad day. Nathan doesn't know this, but I took it, too. He attributed my deep sleep on those nights to the exhaustion we swam in every day, that flavored our food and colored our conversations, and shadowed our looks at ourselves in the mirror.

I got him through kindergarten, mostly by volunteering in the classroom and spending my hours there at Dan's side, watching for the signs he was about to strike. I learned to predict his outbursts by recognizing a glaze that came into his eyes, catching his arm or reining in his foot with mine. I was determined that he stay in school, be as much as possible like other kids, even if it took all my time and energy. He did not ask to be born, as angry children themselves so often say. I willed it, spent a modest fortune, made my body do hormonal tricks. Sitting through kindergarten with him seemed trivial by comparison. But by the school year's end, I knew that I could not do another year this way, or the series of years, or the lifetime, that caring for Dan seem to portend. There had to be another way, an answer, a situation or a new drug or person or procedure. We told the school district we planned home schooling. The assistant principal nodded and signed my permission form to do so without the usual array of questions.

*

This is a story about change, but not Dan's. Dan grew dark and lovely like Nathan, looking for all the world like the overbred, overindulged white children of prosperity you see everywhere. He continued to hit and bite and poke and kick without knowing he was going to. The only change he manifested was a growing strength. During the first grade, when we hired a tutor to come to the house, we started using a cuff jacket with Dan, a sort of modified straight-jacket that kept his hands at his waist. He banged and bruised his head instead, as though only the violence could give his life expressive purpose. I tried teaching him to dance one summer, thinking a creative physical outlet might rechannel his destructive drives. He put his fist through our rec room's sheetrock.

This is a story instead about all the things I thought and tried, and what happened when they failed. Dan's one mercy to me was a regular need for a nap in the afternoon, during which at first I read psychiatric textbooks and journals, and as the years wore on and nothing came of this research, comic books about mutants and government handbooks on vocational counseling. Dan's mutant gift was his indifference to fear, to reprisals for his violence. I imagined speculative universes where he could team up with pink-haired girls conjuring hurricanes, and cyborgs walking through walls, and with them save the free world.

Looking up from these comic books one day, I had an idea that made my hair stand on end: teach Dan to box. Why not give his energies a center stage outlet? The boxing instructor we hired, however, had to put Dan into a full nelson and pin him to the floor in order to stop Dan's furious flailing. Our psychiatrist later said that inviting him to box was like running too much electricity through an erratic circuit.

The circuit didn't perform better; it simply performed more erratically, at a more powerful level. I threw out all the comic books.

Nathan and I then combed the vocational handbooks for jobs for Dan. He never shouted or cursed, so he might become a servant voice one day, a radio announcer, a receptionist. There would be the gauntlet of people to run, going to work, interacting with supervisors and co-workers, but perhaps a guide could be found, perhaps a guide dog could be trained, one who would mouth & lick Dan, ever so lightly and helpfully, before he struck. Nathan and I would stir each other from sleep with ideas for Dan's future, all larded up with if-onlys as far as our own comic-book universe would let us.

I should say something more here about Nathan, who was as much a model of desperate patience and anguished paternal love as anyone in life or literature. Maybe he took a victim's pleasure in it, I don't know. You can see into someone else's soul, even a husband's, only so far. But he got disability leave for a few months each year to help me with Dan, and instead of disappearing into his work as some fathers in his circumstances might have, Nathan instead came home early, stood by me, cried all the same tears that I did, and validated every one of my attempts and failures. He was the heaven to my Dan-filled hell, one of the two huge things I didn't know why I had.

*

The summer of Dan's eighth year gave us too much rain, rotting the nascent apples right off the trees, supercharging the bug life of our neighborhood. Then there'd be night fogs, thick and dangerous; un-used to them, inhabitants of our town drove into trees and ditches and each other in unprecedented numbers. The river, however, roared hap-pily, and the ponds and lakes brimmed and shimmered. It was a perfect summer to drown, though thanks to incessant warnings from the local authorities, no one did through July.

It was also the summer that three things happened for Dan. One, he tortured our dog by putting ticks on her to watch them swell. The sec-ond involved television. We discovered that if Dan watched fish tank videos, he would stay quiet for hours. We tried buying and setting up a real aquarium, thinking its ambient magic would calm Dan's chaos, but no. It had to be the video. Nathan spliced multiple copies of the hour-long video onto an eight-hour tape, so that eight hours of sedation was available for Dan's pleasure. We couldn't figure out immediately how this discovery might reflect or determine a good new direction for Dan, but we felt sure it had to be a positive sign. Dan's psychiatrist thought so, too, though new MRIs and PET scans showed no relevant changes.

I have to say that by eight years old, in spite of his terrible disability, Dan liked math, was fluent in the science spoken by the cohort of doc-tors around him, could play "Amazing Grace" on a wooden flute, and invented a peanut butter cookie bar recipe that included crushed red pepper flakes, maraschino cherries, chickpea flour. He also wore braces on his wrists and hands to support all the bones there he'd repeatedly broken in hitting everyone and everything, and had to submit to a half-hour of ice massage every day to keep down the swelling, since the anti-inflammatories that helped people with arthritis and other pains did nothing for Dan.

Eventually, doctors said, if he kept breaking the irritated bones, they would start failing to heal. He had a plate in his skull from when he'd thrashed himself to the floor and cracked it during a long session in his cuff jacket, and a permanent bend in one leg where a child he'd kicked broke that leg with a chair. I was easily riveted by television shows about parents caring for conjoined twins, Down's syndrome, cerebral palsy, autism, accident, paralysis. It all looked easier that what faced Nathan and me, and Dan. A medical engineer fashioned for Dan a jacket with pulleys and springs that ratcheted Dan's arms if he moved quickly, only permitting slow and gradual movement. The jacket made him look like a Frankenstein monster. He hated wearing it, and it worked only if there were no walls for Dan to smash or furniture to kick over. We bought padded furniture and had tiny caged halogen ceiling lights installed.

Nathan has a coworker who raised her only child, a daughter, to college age, in spite of the fact that the girl had such a severe allergy to peanuts that even a lick of something even vaguely peanutty would puff her face and close her throat. This coworker and her husband shielded their daughter for eighteen years, sent her to school with special lunches, became expert at asking the precise dietary questions and detecting the foods most likely to have the most innocent quantities of peanut dust or peanut oil. The daughter herself learned the same drills. But in her freshman year of college, she ate from a pan of cookies made by a dorm friend, afterward felt woozy and fatigued, went up to her room to lie down, and died. The cookies had chocolate chips in them made with peanut oil. The parents now travel the country pushing for better food labeling laws.

Last slide: there's a variety of lobelia, a delicate white flower, in the high rainforests of Maui that grows nowhere else in the world. It is dying. The Nature Conservancy, which oversees and controls access to the acres where the last sprig of it lives, says that while they'll do what they can to preserve the species, sometimes nature gives up on the things it makes. Sometimes these things seem insufficient, as though their Maker had a headache the day of their creation, or a distracting grief, or lacked the determination to get it right. When these things die, they fold under the soil, and the nutrients of their rot foster the emergence of something new. Something, one hopes, with a better set of chances.

*

Early on the day Dan died, I discovered twelve ticks on the dog, so strategically placed I knew Pepper hadn't got them under her flowing black fur by herself. The ticks were of varying sizes, indicating they had attached at different times. The biggest one had swollen to the size of a raisin. Pepper wiggled and scratched as I sorted through her fur, but the ticks had been placed just where she'd be unable to get at them. She whimpered as I plucked them out when they stood on end, and by the time I had my tweezers on the seventh tick, I didn't even wipe at the tears running down my face. All animal suffering by human hands seemed to accuse me through every one of Pepper's yelps. It took me an hour to get every tick and then to dab each hole with disinfectant. When I was done, Pepper pressed against my knees and licked my face.

I found Dan in front of the aquarium video, his braced hands and wrists turned up slack in his lap, his mouth open a little, staring at the television.

"Dan, honey," I said from the doorway, revealing nothing of the anger I had waiting in my throat. "Get into your cuff jacket, please—I want to talk to you about something."

Dan flailed both arms at me without taking his eyes from the television, as though his arms were guardian serpents with minds of their own, but he let me strap him into it without protest. Our psychiatrist had suggested the cuff jacket for all conversations, pleasant or troubling, partly as a way to get him to focus, and partly, of course, to protect us. How, I had begun wondering lately, were we going to get him into this jacket at ten years old? When he was rebelling at fourteen? At twenty?

We went to the kitchen table. Dan swung his head at the rounded corner of the stove before sitting down but missed. His face bore a patchwork of reddish new scars and whitish older ones, but I still marveled at the raw fact of his presence in the world, this pale-skinned, black-maned being who was my son. I could tell from the jerking of his eyes that he was experiencing withdrawal from the video, and his arms kept straining at their cuffs.

Sometimes it helped to get right to the point. "I noticed something strange about Pepper this morning," I said. "She had a dozen ticks on her, in places that seemed arranged. Did you have anything to do with this?"

Dan's dark eyes came out of their spin. "I was doing an experiment," he said. One thing about Dan: he never lied. "I read about them in a book and heard that when they suck they grow big. I wanted to see that."

"Dan, they made Pepper miserable, and what's more, they have diseases! She might die!"

The tunnel of his eyes reminded me of someone looking at me with binoculars. "I don't care," he said, shrugging.

I stood up so fast the chair screeched out from under me. We were not to spank Dan, as it did nothing but overstimulate him, but I couldn't stop myself from grabbing him by his strapped-down arm and shaking him. Then I pulled the cinches on his cuffs as tight as they would go, got him on his feet, and started him in the direction of his "Respite Room," a walk-in closet without windows, really, that was entirely padded, in which we placed Dan for discipline. All psychiatrist approved, of course. I almost had him there, inside its marshmallow haven.

But a recent growth spurt had given him strength I never expected from an eight-year-old. He slammed into my chest with one shoulder, knocking the wind out of me, and when I bent over with a gasp, he squatted and sprang, hitting me square in the face with the top of his head. Then he was gone, kicking open the screen door, his footsteps clapping down the walk.

I caught my breath after a sickening interval. With tentative fingertips I discovered a forehead knot, but amazingly, no bloody nose. A roughened cheek and sore eyebrow would result in my twelfth black eye. Beyond the physical injuries, and in that moment, not so different from them, the most abject misery welled up from every single one of my cells, as though the grief and sorrow and anguish of the eight long years with Dan underwent an instant seismic liquefaction. Given tear ducts instead of pores, my whole body would have cried. I sat folded on the kitchen floor for a long time, holding myself.

It was late morning. Nathan was at work. I got up and went looking for Dan. Two knowing neighbors pointed the way they had seen Dan run, toward the pond at the end of our street. It was really just a pool off the river, but it was wide and deep enough to warrant a dock and ladder for water play or fishing. Rimmed by firs and maples that kept out most sunlight, the pond was a broody place even at midday. Dan was never allowed there alone, but he seemed to respond to its uncomplicated silence. Both Nathan and I had taken solitary walks to its banks, looking for whatever anyone looks for in deep, reflective water, or in a wood fire, or in a clear, moonless night sky.

Standing at the dock with his back to me, Dan in his cuff jacket was a white shape against the dark water. He didn't turn until he heard my feet on the dock, and then he whirled. "I hate you," he said. "I hate that I'm alive, and it's all your fault."

"You're right," I said. "It is my fault. I did make you come alive. Me and your daddy both. God, too, some people would say."

His pale, scarred face contorted. "I would *kill* you. I *would*."

I had no more capacity for shock. Beached by the tumult, I could only stare at Dan in detached amazement. "I know it is so, so hard for you, Dan. I know you must be frustrated."

"You think you've done me a big favor," he shouted, his arms writhing, his wrists beginning to bleed from sawing against the tight cuffs. "You think you're so *good*."

"I'm just doing the best I can," I said quickly. "I don't know what else to do."

"Well, you're bad. Know how I know? Look at me. Could someone good have made someone like me?"

"Oh, Danny," I said, reaching for him. But with the same sort of feline spring he'd made against my chest, Dan twisted and leaped toward the pond, slipped, and struck his head so hard against the dock that it sounded like an axe against a hollow tree. He bounced unconscious into the pond, so full the dock barely cleared its surface. Wavelets raced to the wooded shoreline.

This is the third thing that happened to Dan that summer. I let him be right. I let him sink, though I'm easily a good enough swimmer to have gone after him. I let his last thought be that he had a bad mother. "I am bad," I said to the stilling water. "Bad. Bad."

*

The cards, letters, flowers, casseroles, Bibles, and even the offer of a new puppy came from a wider array of friends and strangers than I thought possible. The outpouring of sympathy had in it the energy and warmth of relief, as though only in dying could Dan finally give the local community something uncomplicated to feel about him. We got offers of stays at Umbrian villas or Hawaiian condos from Dan's doctors and a wealthy widow at the edge of town whom we'd never met. The coroner, after gently informing us that our son was dead, sent his wife over with a ham. The sheriff and volunteer firefighter who dredged Dan up from the pond and questioned me perfunctorily afterward visited together a few days later with their wives, bearing a hamper of berry pies and meat loaf. The last school Dan had attended made him a giant card which all the students signed. This time it was Nathan who couldn't rise from bed, as I had lain stricken and thinking after the second miscarriage. I met all the visitors and wrote all the thank-you notes and declined all the offers of puppies, villas, and condos. Something of Dan's hardness entered me when he died, drying my eyes and steeling my spine for the torrent of well-meaning sympathy.

Nathan slept through most of the month's bereavement leave given him by his employers. When he awoke, he displayed Dan-like impatience, annoyance, mood swings that I'd never seen in him before. In addition to Dan's hardness, I also seemed to acquire a measure of his fearlessness and his indifference. Nathan and I argued over nothing. We broke dishes, cried noisily. I went for long walks in the middle of the night, my feet oozing with blisters when I came home. Nathan scuffled with a stranger at the grocery store. I heard about it later from the sheriff, who was called in to break it up. Though we dismantled the "Respite Room" of its wall padding, I went inside it often in those first weeks after Dan's death. When he thought me out of earshot, Nathan took to hitting our bed rhythmically with a tennis racket, the way some therapists counsel people in crisis to safely dispense their anger. In spite of the care Nathan took to conceal it from me, I could hear the distant chant of his *no, no, no,* every time the racket struck the bed.

*

I've read that many couples who lose an only child divorce, but Nathan and I were not among them. After weeks and months of grieving, Nathan and I grew quiet. For weeks and months after that, we moved with the caution that usually identifies the very old. Nathan went back to work. I repainted the entire inside of the house. Pepper the dog developed an odd, occasional limp.

We got used to the well-wishing mourners who came unbidden to our door, and then we got used to the silence when they stopped. Only one woman came every Sunday to throw flowers on the pond, one of the playground assistants named Jan from when Dan was in second grade. She had dyed blonde hair that showed a length of brown roots and a round, kind face. She might have been anywhere between twenty-five and forty. At first she came to the door and asked me if we wanted to go with her, and I did, a time or two. When I began to refuse, she went alone, and continued doing so every week; I could tell from the carnations rotting in the pond shoreline, or on the ice when the pond froze over in January. One Sunday, I called to her as she walked from her parked car to the pond. "Please stop," I said. She smiled sadly, but continued on.

"Well," Nathan said, when I complained about it. "She's not doing anything wrong, exactly."

"It's ghoulish," I said. "It's weird and vicarious."

Nathan had evolved a slow, tentative smile since Dan, as though he wanted to be careful of what he smiled about and why. "Yes, it is weird and vicarious. All mourning is."

I knew Nathan was right, but it didn't stop me from starting to swim in the pond as early in the spring as I could, when things thawed, on the Sunday afternoons Jan came to throw her flowers. I'd be breast stroking around the pond, so cold it took my breath away. Jan would be there with her blonde-brown hair, wrapped in chunky sweaters, cradling her flowers and murmuring to herself. I stared up from the black water, daring her to throw out her carnations, always yellow. She'd throw, and I'd glare and splash.

"Ask her for dinner sometime," Nathan offered once when I came home quivering with cold and anger. And then he considered it. "On second thought, don't. Forget I said that."

"Don't you have any children of your own?" I said to her from the water the next Sunday. An old snow lay around the pond's edge. My legs and arms had ached themselves numb in the icy water. I knew I'd never wear the wetsuit Nathan bought and laid out on my side of the bed without a word. The pond at its deepest point was forty-eight feet—I knew that from the sheriff's dredging report. New "No Lifeguard on Duty" signs had appeared in recent weeks on both sides of the dock.

Jan, whose last name I could never remember, paused at the dock's edge. Her face got the hurt shock of a slapped child. Then an adult measure of pique and cunning crept in. "You think this just belongs to you," she said, peeling the carnations one by one out of their cheap supermarket wrapping and tossing them in the water around me. "You think you're the only one who's sad."

"Oh, no," I said. "There's enough sadness to go around for everyone. I was just wondering why you have to go looking for it in other people's lives."

"You think I don't know about what you did," she said. "You think we all don't know."

I caught in a breath, so that when I stopped treading water I didn't sink—not immediately. Then I swam to the dock, hoisted myself out, and faced her, dripping. Only wearing a ragged red swimsuit, I could not control my shaking, nor the coarse flare of gooseflesh on my arms and legs. "What the hell do you know," I said. "You have absolutely no idea, no idea whatsoever."

It had been some months. No one had ever come forward about what I had not done. I stared into Jan's round, petulant face, gauging it for insight, for malice, for wisdom. There was no one I had told. Only the pond and the reeds knew. I looked back at them, and then again at Jan. Then I felt something long coiled in me ease. I could give this woman the truth, and give up my claims on sympathy forever. There would be a purity in it, a perfection, a blessed reckoning. I had my mouth open to make the confession. I started to smile. Dan's ghostly face seemed to smile back up from the pond bottom.

Jan's expression flickered for a moment but returned to its angry set. "You—you didn't let him be normal. You took him out of school. You made him be an only child. There's something wrong with the natural way of things here. And—and it's never the kid's fault. If you ask me, that little boy never had a chance."

My lips could barely move. "I didn't ask you."

"I know it." She fondled and then strew her last carnation. "So you just let me have my little flowers, and maybe I'll leave off with my opinions." She turned and padded back down the dock.

"Let me tell you what really happened," I said, hurrying after her.

"Don't." Jan said as she got into her car. "I already know what I know."

I ran home in my wet sneakers and towel, strings of wet hair whipping my neck. Nathan was watching a golf tournament on TV. "I need to tell you what happened that day with Dan," I said, still out of breath.

Nathan's face softened. "Go take your bath. You're probably hypothermic. Was that woman there again?"

I sat down on the ottoman at his feet, soaking its fabric with my wet rump. "I could have saved Dan," I said. "But I didn't."

He gave me a wintry smile from way back inside himself. "We've been over and over this. Honey, please, take your bath. I thought we'd go out to dinner. To that bar that you like, with the burgers. Hurry. The roads are icing."

"Why won't you let me talk to you?"

"Stop blaming yourself. If we're going to have a life now, we have to forgive ourselves and move forward. Everyone says so. The therapists we pay say so."

"What kind of a life can you have when you're responsible for someone else's death?"

Nathan shook his head as if I were a dense high school girl. "Honey, it's over. You can't bring Dan back to life by flaying yourself with the circumstances of his death." He got up, lifted me to my feet, and drew me toward the bathroom. "Come on. Your lips are blue. Bathtime. Let me pour you some wine while you soak."

I went. I let him undress me like a child, glance at my nude body without interest, and help me into the tub. The hot water roiled and steamed as the tub filled, the herbal bubble-bath heaping into mountains and icebergs. Nathan dimmed the lights and went for my wine. I watched the square of his shoulders disappear around the corner.

I couldn't have created a better man myself. We would be together till one of us buried the other, beside Dan, in the town cemetery. Friends and family alike would remark on our mutual devotion. Our collective mark on the world now only required our perfect union. So I told it to the churning bathwater pouring from the tap, from our well, no doubt a kindred source for the pond. "I let Dan die," I whispered to the water, which in its kindness said nothing back.

2 What Really Happened

No one could explain it. Every morning for a week in early summer we'd arrive at the nursery and find all the *Pinus lambertiana* seedlings grouped together in the center courtyard. The first time it happened the yard workers put them back without comment, assuming someone had arranged them that way intentionally and then had forgotten them. But it happened again the next day, and the next. Whoever got to the nursery first would greet everyone else with a puzzled, amused face and say, *there they are again.* Other nursery employees said, oh, it's probably just kids, bored kids on summer vacation.

But the night I lay with Larry out in the park bushes, I thought about the infant sugar pines, imagined them crawling on tiny root filament feet back into their group even as we lay there. After a couple of weeks, their mysterious movement stopped. I wondered about it for a long time, even after the summer was over and Larry and his wife were gone.

We worked together at the nursery, Larry and me. I ran the register, and he was one of the yard workers who drove the forklift, moving sacks of peat and ornamental bark. Summer job for me, in between semesters of graduate botany. He was supposed to be writing his dissertation in philosophy. His wife, also a philosophy student, was away a lot that summer. He and I would sit on the creaky wooden porch of his rented house after work and talk late into the nights. He told me about growing up in rural Tennessee, where he lived next door to an uncle who had visions. I told him about learning to drive in Los Angeles, about flying on planes—things he had never done. Me being a wonder to someone was a wonder in itself.

And we talked about marriage. Mostly, Larry would say how foolish it was. I'd lived with a guy back in California for a while, which wasn't quite the same, though I still had the china we had bought together. As I listened to Larry complain, I offered what I could of support and advice, but I finally started to hear something else in the complaints about his wife. He wanted more, something bigger, grander. A woman who knew something of the world, who was wise and sophisticated. Who turned out to be me.

We finally devoured each other in July. He said the kinds of things to me that only sound dumb and corny if they're not said to you: *I can't live without you. I want to leave town with you. You're a fine-looking woman.* I let him convince me that he'd be doing his wife a favor by leaving her. And though I said, OK, but no sex, not until you're officially separated, I did let him kiss me, lift me off my feet out by the park one night and carry me into the bushes. He was big and supple, and he lay me in the grass like heavy treasure. I'd forgotten what it was like to kiss someone for hours. It started to rain while we were lying there, bright lightning flickering like candlelight, heavy drops pattering on the leaves around us. He said, it's a good sign: richness and wetness and fertility.

When his wife returned, the two of them went back to Tennessee, where both of them were from, to be with their families while they divided the spoils of their marriage. He called me, frightened, and from my telephone distance I tried to calm him. *Things will be all right,* I'd say. He'd call me several times a day and leave one message after another on my answering machine. When we talked, he'd read poems he had written to me and describe the roads he'd learned to drive on. He promised to show it all to me someday. Once he sang me a soft love song, tinny over the phone wires. I cried—how stupid—but it was so sweet. So tender and ridiculous and unreal.

One day I didn't hear from him at all. And the next he called at six in the morning. He didn't even say hello. His voice was low. "Are you ready for this?" he said.

"Ready?—is it time?" I wasn't quite awake, but I was trying to sound like I was.

"Cass, I'm not ready to leave her. I can't. I want you too much."

"What?" That woke me. "Larry, that makes no sense."

"Cass, look, I can't leave her. I'm sorry. She's—she's here. I know her. Everyone knows her. Do you understand?"

"No, I don't." I smelled myself in bed: warm, sleepy. The whole pallid day stretched out in front of me, leaking in the window. The silence was taut like breath held in the dark. "Well, go then," I said. "Stop wasting your phone money." It sounded harsh. "Oh, God, Larry."

"I know, Cass."

I didn't hear from him again. A couple of weeks went by. I saw empty spaces everywhere, heard something mourning in simple conversations, but I kept my thoughts to myself, close and tight inside. It was quieter at the nursery. The other yard worker drove the forklift. Thank God, I kept saying to myself, weary, newly sophisticated, thank God I hadn't fucked him, thinking the word "fucked" and savoring its cold, brisk consonants. Though I couldn't quite put out of my mind the greedy look on his face and the bend of his neck as he leaned over me and flicked each breast lightly with his teeth.

Early one Saturday morning, almost three weeks later, the phone rang. It was a beautiful, oddly cool and dry midwestern summer morning. A pair of Carolina wrens sang their bubbly, nervous duet over and over. I lay in bed, watching the light select leaves to land on. The air-conditioning compressors outside the apartment next door went on and off, sucking in their breaths and blowing them out hot.

I picked up the phone. It was Larry's wife, with her soft Tennessee accent. Immediately my body went on the alert, tightening my mouth and closing in on my breath. I sat up in bed. I wanted to tell her quickly, you know, nothing happened between your husband and me. A man and a woman flirt—it means nothing. We didn't sleep together.

"Um, Cass?" she said. "Cass?"

"I'm here, Rainey." It was strange already. Even beyond the awkwardness of me speaking to her, I could feel something wrong. Like the voices of policemen calling in the night, saying, ma'am, I'm sorry but your son has been killed. In a bar fight. In a wreck. Fallen from the quarry ledge, hitting his head on the side, drowning.

"Cass, I'm sorry to be bothering you, but can you come down here?"

I felt suddenly lost. Where is here? Where I am is in my house, with my things. "Where are you, Rainey? What's going on?"

"Um, I know it's a lot to ask, but Larry's been asking for you. Can you come?"

Hearing his name made me suddenly very focused, careful. He loomed up between us, watching us, silent. I resolved not to look at him but peered around him instead. "What is going on," I said. I put an edge in my voice. Not a question this time, but a flat demand.

"Well, Larry's gone and shot himself, but he didn't die."

Sudden panic choked me. "Jesus, Rainey, is he all right? My God, why did he do that?" I remembered, oddly, a moment back in that passionate week. Larry's long arms were around me, across my chest, holding me to him while he stood behind me. My hands were in a bowl of cherries, pitting them. We were making a pie. My nails turned purple; they would stay purple for days. I put up the dripping red fingers to stroke him, only catching myself inches before they reached his hair. He took one of my hands and put the fingers in his mouth, sucking the cherry juice from them.

Rainey was steady. "He's home now, not hurt too bad. He's not much with guns, you know?"

Actually I didn't know. I knew only some things about Larry: that he had a quick laugh, was writing a dissertation on Nietzsche, had a knife-fight scar under one arm. His father owned a bar. His eyes were long-lashed, almost girlish, and he often fell silent in groups and played with his hair. Useless information. I searched around—what did I know that would explain this? His hands were big around the handles of a wheelbarrow.

I tried to stop the tumbling of my thoughts. "Look, Rainey, I don't know what I could do there." Even though he was married, he had sworn it wouldn't be for long. I had thought I knew what I was doing. Everything was going to work out. But it was a mistake. A mistake. Something to forget about. Something to pretend I never did.

"I know, I know." She'd been expecting my resistance. "But he's asking for you." Her voice cracked on the "asking."

I went. I wanted to be a good person, you see. That's what got me. I let her give me directions—it was about three hours south, not far inside the Tennessee border, down winding roads that I barely saw as I passed over them. Green, lots of leaves. Someone calm might have said, pretty country. Out of my fog I saw the big, white-on-green signs shouting out the road names I had written down on my scratch paper, in letters guided by Rainey's voice.

I got there just before noon. Actually I got to the turnoff for Larry's family's house before noon. I was hungry. I hadn't eaten breakfast, just showered and put on clothes and gotten in the car. There was a Mighty Burger on the corner of the turnoff, next to a gas station and a little market. I went in, got a burger to go, and sat outside in my car to eat it. Men in overalls went in and came out, carrying their white paper bags. Women with babies sat in the restaurant, talking and handing pieces of meat to their children. An Amish buggy went by, the blond children looking curiously at me as I sat and ate. I usually have an urge to hide myself, avoid people's eyes, when I eat alone, as if there were something shameful about it. Satisfying hunger seems less primal when it's done with someone. But I looked right back at the Amish kids. I was reckless, chewing my food by myself, right in front of everyone. Three men in a pickup truck went by and waved at me.

I went back into the restaurant to wash my face and hands. There was no one in the bathroom. I washed my face several times, stalling for time. My face in the mirror was wet, but pretty. I looked critically at its fine shape, the large green eyes, small, soft chin, high forehead. What had Larry seen in this face that made him want to leave his wife? Had that anything to do with why he had shot himself?

"Come on," I said to my reflection, watching it pucker up with scorn. "You're not that gorgeous, Cass." I bent closer to the mirror. There were little zits on my forehead, a mole on my jaw, wrinkles starting under my eyes. I started picking blackheads, squeezing hard, making my eyes water. When I went outside and got back in the car, my nose was red and a little puffy in the mirror.

The dust rolled with my car into the clearing where Larry's family lived. Their house was a straight-sided white and tan trailer, out of which additional rooms grew at right angles. Rainey had told me to look for the junked green Pontiac parked nearby. It was there, up to its fading fenders in deep summer grass and reddish mud.

I got out. It was quiet and cool, though the sun was pale and fierce. The steep hills around me were thick with lurid, summer-green maples, oaks, and dogwood. They leaned in together darkly, cutting the place off from the road that took me there. The sun probably hit the ground for only a few hours a day. Right then it was glinting off the trailer roof.

I slammed the car door, hard. I wanted someone to hear me, to come out and say, *we were expecting you. Won't you come in.* I wanted the family to thank me for driving all that way, offer me lemonade, tell me how much it meant for Larry to see me. I knew Larry's mother was a nice woman. She was the only one in his family he really liked. His father was short-tempered and didn't say much. They would take me in to see Larry, who would weep when he saw me. We would all be embarrassed, but I would say, it's just trauma, I used to assist in an emergency room, it's not uncommon for the tears to come, for the man to cry like a child.

No one came out of the trailer. There was no sound from it at all. A bird song I didn't recognize came from somewhere in the trees, an angry skitter that was immediately answered by another one far away. I wondered if I had gone to the right trailer. If I hadn't, I would need directions to the right one anyway, so I knocked on the door. Besides, I wanted to see someone right then, anyone.

I heard footsteps, and then the door opened. It was Larry. One side of his face and neck, including the eye, was wrapped in thick white gauze, the kind we used to layer on wounds in the emergency room. The skin I could see around the bandage was ruddy, as if badly sun-burned. He squinted. He couldn't put his glasses on around the mound of the bandage, so he couldn't identify me quickly. I felt weak. I wanted to take his hands and put them on my face so he would know me.

"Cass?" he finally said. "Cass. What in the hell are you doing here?" It wasn't anger exactly. The tone was more indignant, as if I'd found a secret hiding place, a treehouse or a fort, and entered without permission.

The part of me that was uncoiling to reach for him retracted quickly. Wait. I thought you needed me. I went over the call from Rainey that morning. She had called. Yes. I had the directions she gave me over the phone written down on the sweaty note I held in my hand. I looked up at him, at the one eye I could see.

"Rainey called, said you had—said you hurt yourself?"

He put a hand up to the bandage, pressing it. I heard his fingers scratch on the porous gauze. "Well, you can see for yourself, can't you?"

"She said you needed me." I stepped back, spreading my feet, bal-ancing myself. You'd never think one eye could glare so. I felt like I'd given a wrong answer. "No, I mean, she said you asked for me." Yes—that was what she said. I stared back into that cold blue-gray eye, mus-tering a chilly look of my own, tensing my jaw. Though I hadn't forgot-ten the touch of his mouth with its rough teeth, and the spongy ten-derness of his hands. It was crazy and I knew it, but I wanted to lay him down somewhere and kiss around the bandage. "So here I am."

I still thought then that I was being a good person. And I thought that being a good person meant you did what other people wanted you to do, and that their wishing it of you was insurance against error. I had Rainey's request around me like a nimbus.

"Rainey wouldn't do that," he said, matter-of-factly.

"Well, for God's sake, Larry, I wouldn't have come here otherwise."

"I don't know about that, Cass. You seem to like meddling in other people's lives. Getting between them. Saying things you have no busi-ness saying." He blinked and winced as the bandage and whatever lay beneath it caught him in his anger and pinched him.

I started to feel a cold, greasy sweat seep out of me. I took a step back from the trailer with Larry looming out of it like a watchdog. He's crazed. Drugged up on painkillers. I remembered my role: I'm a visiting friend, and I have to be patient with him. "Hey, come on," I said. "I'm just sorry you're hurt."

"I suppose she told you how it happened," he said. "Well, at least get that straight and then go back to where you came from."

"What happened?"

"I got drunk."

I held my breath. The truth—here it comes. If it had nothing to do with me, I'd be off the hook. Innocent. But if it did, then—well, then, what happened between Larry and me mattered somehow. But, God, how awful, to measure a thing's worth by how much pain it causes! Like some kind of abusive experiment on animals: if the solution burns rabbit eyes, the acid's strong enough. What in the hell was I thinking?

"You know how the lighter fluid cans say Do Not Squirt into Open Flame? Do you know why? The flame goes up the stream of fluid right into the can. Then it blows up. Can shrapnel everywhere." He jabbed a finger toward where his eye would be under the bandage. "This eye is blind now, Cass."

It was my fault—God, I was to blame for his rage and his carelessness. Wasn't I? I had to touch him, to lay my hands on him. Please, let me heal it and make it right. I went toward the trailer door. I reached out and put my fingers around his wrist, squeezing it. He stood there, gaping down at me in surprise. Then he smiled, a strange, twisted grin. Aha—he did care. I smiled back at him, knowing that my face looked loving, warm. Oh, good—some things can be forgiven.

The grin left him as quickly as it had come, and without saying anything more Larry turned up the stairs and went into the trailer. The door slammed behind him, rattling the aluminum siding and loose window frames. I waited. He would probably come back soon. I shifted on my feet. I felt like a Girl Scout selling cookies, waiting for the housewife to get her purse, trying not to seem like a stranger standing there, unwanted. The sun was burning my neck. I waited. A plane went by overhead, very high, its contrail a blurry stripe in the hot blue sky. It was going west. I wanted to be on it the way you want a drink of water when you're feverish. I wanted to be anywhere else.

If only I could get back in my car, prickly, ashamed of my pale thighs in the car seat, and drive away as fast as possible. The way I came. I turned to my car—how I loved that car! At the twist of my touch it flamed alive, ready, humming, waiting for my direction. I could scream inside it and no one would hear me. That car knew all my secrets. Once I decided that if I ever committed suicide I would do it in my car. Let it crush me with its metallic gasoline embrace.

But before I could get the door open and myself inside, another car came slowly down the stony dirt drive. I should have just left right then, waving solemnly the way people in the country wave to each other when they pass on the backroads: one hand up, fingers slightly apart.

But I didn't. It was Rainey and an older woman who looked a little like her; I assumed it was her mother. Or an older sister maybe. I never did find out. This older woman had on a black-and-white checked dress, and she stared at me as she got out of the car and went into the trailer. Rainey didn't follow her in. She stood on the far side of the car, the spaces where her eyes should have been big and hollow with sunglasses. She was very pretty: smooth hair boyish short, bright lipstick, small hands and feet. Compact. The kind of woman I felt rangy and clumsy next to. I'd only met her a couple of times; she was quiet, seemed self-contained, and studied conversational Greek.

I couldn't tell if she was looking at me or not. "Did he talk to you?" she asked.

"What?"

She made a gesture with her hand. Oh, yeah. How could you possibly know, it seemed to say. You outsider. "He hasn't said a thing since it happened," she said. "I was hoping that seeing you would get him talking again."

"Wait a minute. I thought he asked for me."

She turned her face away and rubbed the back of her short hair. "I figured that would get you down here." She paused, took a breath. "I'm real sorry, Cass, but he was just lying there, for hours, not talking. He would hum sometimes, though."

My face worked, as if I had something in my mouth. Rainey came over to me. "What did he say to you?"

She was very close. I smelled her perfume: lemony something. It made me feel sick.

"How did he shoot himself?" I said.

She took one hand with the other, holding it. "It's really private family business," she said. I could see an eye squinting through the sunglasses. "He was pointing it—somewhere, at someone"—she cleared her throat here—"and then he looked down the barrel."

"Really," I said. "Well, he told me that he tripped and fell on a pole, right up the eye." I stuck an imaginary pole into my own eye for effect.

Years and years later, I would still wake up early in the morning, just at dawn, when the first birds would start their conversations, and think about those words I said then to Rainey, and what my face must have looked like saying them. I would imagine all kinds of scenarios in which I said other things, mild vanilla things that I would have forgotten that same day. Probably other thoughts would torment me instead in the trembling morning hours. But the sneer of that lie echoes down my dreams to this day. I'm still not sure why I said it. I guess I wanted to impose my own version of reality on things, even if I had to make it up.

Rainey stiffened, seeming to grow much taller. "Liar," she said. Her voice was even, her jaw like granite. "Fuck you, Cass," she spat. She backed away from me, her mouth contorted. She turned and disappeared into the trailer.

Plants do a version of screaming, if you take the trouble to hook them up to a scope that measures their surges of starches. They react to people who pull on them, to dogs that eat them. As I got in my car, keeping my face still, my own leaves steady, a spasm tore through me, whining like hot wind through the tunnels of my body. I bumped my head on the door, jamming a key up one of my fingernails. All the while I kept hearing the words: fuck you, Cass, fuck you, Cass. Over and over. I rolled up the window and stabbed the key at the ignition, missing twice. I finally found it, turned the key too many times, hearing the starter grind, a shriek. Oh, joy—what a relief when the car finally moved, my foot on the pedal pushing it and me away from this hot little hole in the trees and the trailer shimmering like a greasy quarter and Rainey's voice screaming, screaming, in my ears, and everything behind me dwindling and blurring with dust in my rearview mirror as I lurched down the road.

I drove and turned and got lost, shaking. I finally stopped in front of a long fence with sheep behind it, watching me, blinking. As I sat there, hearing the valves in the engine clattering, feeling my nose running, really not knowing where in the hell I was, I wondered what had happened to Larry. The only thing I knew for sure was that he had his head wrapped. Why—I hadn't a clue. There were three versions of the thing: his, mine, and Rainey's. It was like an experiment that three people had written up and gotten completely different. They get you in the lab for tampering with evidence, but everyone does it, even professors. Go back to the experiment and change what happened. If you just clump this cell next to the others—easy, careful with the pipette—you can declare a trend in turnip genetics. I'd never done it, though. I had been such a purist. I wanted things to happen the way I wanted them to on their own.

This is the way the summer ended: I promise. No goofing around with facts. I got home early that evening after asking a nice woman shelling peas on her porch how to get back to the highway. I went to work at the nursery the next day, looking for Larry everywhere, knowing full well that he would probably never come back to work. I was right. I heard from a mutual friend that Larry and Rainey had withdrawn from the university and were going back to their hometown for a while. Fall came in one September afternoon on a sharp, dry breeze, and I went back to school the next week.

I saw them a few days later. They were sitting on a low limestone wall in front of the town's tiny sculpture park, eating ice cream cones together. I was across and down the street, holding a loaf of bread. I was close enough to see that Larry's face was the same as it was before. No scars—he even rubbed that once-patched eye at one point, carelessly.

I started down the street, intending to go right by them. I got close enough to see that they were wearing old clothes, the kind you wear when you're packing to move. They were talking animatedly as if they had just met each other in a class, or in the park. I started to go even closer, wanting to look in both of Larry's eyes for evidence of the summer, of the extreme people the three of us had been not two months before.

But I froze up and stopped, about twenty feet from them. Larry turned and saw me, and Rainey, following his glance, looked too. Their faces hung there—I can still see them when I close my eyes— without changing expression, looking through me. Then, in perfect unison, they looked away. Erasing me. Or as if I were a sound they thought they heard—but no. Nothing there.

My hands clenched around my bread. I put my free hand up to my face; it was warm, as if sunburned. College kids in khaki shorts and young locals shirted in tie-dye flowed past me on the sidewalk in both directions, talking, laughing, singing to themselves. I stood there for a long moment, swaying in the current. Finally I turned around in my tracks and walked away, back to my car.

Evidence isn't always where you think to look for it. They teach you that in Intro Botany, but like most good lessons, you have to learn it again and again. I opened the glove compartment to stuff in the receipt for the bread, only to find the Mighty Burger bag where I'd crushed it without thinking those weeks ago. And as I drove around a sharp corner the space under the passenger seat spat out the copy of *On Being and Time* that Larry had given me. The odometer remembered the four hundred twenty-six miles the car and I had traveled to get to the shiny trailer in the woods and back. What you do stays done. There was some record. Whether we wanted it or not, there was some record.

3   The Visitor

It had all been very proper. There had been letters between Luz's home in Guadalajara, and Los Angeles, where Diego's family had lived for some years. Diego's parents wanted him to marry a decent Mexicana, not a wild American girl with no morals, and Luz was the daughter of old family friends. Diego traveled to Guadalajara to marry her, and he brought her back to live with him in Los Angeles.

The new couple found a narrow apartment for rent downtown on West 18th Street. The landlord, Mr. Mulzit, lived in the big house across the courtyard. After showing them the apartment, he asked both Luz and Diego for their naturalization papers.

"I don't keep house for no wetbacks," Mr. Mulzit had said, his black eyes fierce under heavy graying brows.

Luz nodded. Agreeing with English speakers, she had found, bought her more time to figure out their clipped words. Wetbacks: *espaldas mojados.*

"I find out there are wetbacks around and I throw everyone right out into the street and call the Immigration," Mr. Mulzit continued.

Immigration: *migra.* Luz nodded, and when she understood she nodded harder. The landlady, Mrs. Mulzit, was standing beside him, holding a white cat. Luz smiled at the cat, wanting to touch it but afraid to.

"We will cooperate with you complete," said Diego. His English was better than Luz's, and he had a princely calm.

"Well, all right then," Mr. Mulzit said. He handed Diego the lease, which Diego bent down to sign on the smooth concrete in the sun. Luz did not like for Diego to be kneeling in the courtyard, signing important papers on the ground. But she said nothing.

"You sign, too," said Mr. Mulzit to Luz when Diego was finished.

"I sign?" The only thing Luz had ever signed before was her marriage license, and she wasn't even sure that counted. Signing things was what men did. She pressed the paper against Diego's back and signed anyway. Her name on that form belonged to the Mulzits now, to Los Angeles, to America. She could never go back and leave no trace.

*

Luz's new life was pleasant enough. While Diego worked as a gardener's assistant, Luz cleaned the apartment, beat the rugs with a broom the way her mother had, and cooked as best she could, even though all the familiar Mexican foods here came in cans and were expensive. She braided her long hair every day to keep it neat—something she hadn't always bothered with when an unmarried girl in Mexico. She bought sturdy, cheap shoes.

Luz even liked the Mulzits. She liked watching them. From her kitchen with its windows on two sides, Luz could see the freeway on one side and into the courtyard on the other. Mr. Mulzit had a garage full of standing power saws, and when he went into it, horrible shrieks came out. Mrs. Mulzit wore an apron over her dresses, fed the cat scraps from a battered foil pan, and pulled weeds from the flowerbeds. Luz began wearing an apron over her dress, too. When Luz's sister-in-law presented Luz with a small rose bush and helped her plant it in the tiny backyard garden plot, Mrs. Mulzit came over and offered suggestions. After that, every time Luz met Mrs. Mulzit outside, they spoke of the roses.

"If they are free of the bugs, roses will grow," said Mrs. Mulzit.

"I pick them off," Luz said. "Diego shows me." Her mouth was careful around the English words.

"That is much work," said Mrs. Mulzit. "Why do you not use the spray?"

Spray? Luz nodded, but did not understand. "Yes, okay," she said. "Spray." She resolved to ask Diego about it later. "You are very right."

She saw Mr. Mulzit bring in a newspaper each afternoon, so she asked Diego to order them a newspaper, too. But the paper Diego got them came in the morning. Luz looked at it every day, though it had more English words than she could manage in a week. She took pleasure even in the words she did not know. Someday she would learn them.

*

One day Diego came home at his usual hour of four in the afternoon and did not kiss her. He would not meet her eyes. For all his solid manliness, Diego was such a boy, Luz thought. Something was wrong that he did not know how to tell her. Sometimes Luz thought that without women, there would be no children and no speech—men had in themselves only part of what was necessary to produce these things.

"How was your work today, Diego?" she sang out in Spanish, as if they were playing and he were trying to hide somewhere she could see.

Instead of avoiding conversation as he usually did—by rummaging around in the refrigerator for a beer and a snack, or washing his hands long and hard as though they had something poisonous on them—Diego sat right down in front of her, across from her chair at the kitchen table from which she often watched the Mulzits. *"Mi amada,"* he said, folding his hands and working them together, "I have agreed to shelter someone." He ducked his head, as if expecting her to hurl something at him. She sat there motionless. "For a fee, of course. We'll get twenty-five dollars for just one night."

"Husband, what are you talking about?" Luz said, though she knew exactly what he meant and a cold shock thrilled her. He had offered to help some *ilegales* by giving them a place to stay their first night across the border. Even Americans who sheltered *ilegales* could find themselves in jail, she knew. And immigrants like her had been sent back to

Mexico with only what they could carry. Everyone from Mexico, *ilegales* or not, knew the stories of the unlucky as well as they knew their own memories.

"It's because we are so trustworthy!" Diego said. "The usual safe house can't possibly shelter anyone for a while, and a father needing money for his family is coming all the way from Torreón. His job in Bakersfield starts in a few days and if he misses the crew leaving—"

But Luz had stopped listening, for she knew she would consent. Partly because Diego wanted it, partly for the money—half a day's wages. And because a very small part of her with a clear voice said, may one not have guests in a free country?

"Here is the money," Diego said, pulling from his pockets wads of one- and five-dollar bills. "My crewmate, Cesar, has given us the money in advance as a display of *buena fe,* the good faith." Diego spoke quickly, as though relieving great pressure. "It is his *tío* Reynaldo who comes. We tell Mr. and Mrs. Mulzit an uncle is coming for a visit. We can say that, yes? It is not lying—he is someone's uncle. We can just say, 'this is Uncle Reynaldo.' We do not have to say whose uncle."

The cramp of fear in Luz's chest must have been visible on her face, for Diego touched her cheek. "Sweet Luzita, it will be all right, it is just this once, and Cesar and the work crew will honor us, and here is this money!"

Luz looked at the clumps on the white tablecloth. Why was all American money that same queasy green? *"Esta bien,"* she said finally. "When does he come?"

"Tomorrow night."

*

The next morning, Luz went to work scrubbing the walls, polishing bathroom fixtures, washing all their clothes—even some clean things hanging in the closet. Then she washed herself, rubbing the coarse washcloth over every inch of her skin, and refilling the tub to wash her long hair. When it was nearly dry she braided it tightly and put on a white dress. Worried that there was something she had missed, she searched the kitchen for grime, or dust, or crumbs but found none. She sat and smoothed her already slick black hair.

Down in the courtyard, Mrs. Mulzit was working on a grapevine, trying to train it onto a trellis. Luz put her apron on over her white dress and went downstairs. The sun was bright and harsh, and shadows seemed to be everywhere. She went to her rose bush, which no longer harbored any insects, since Diego had sprayed it with what she now knew was household insecticide. She had weeded it a few days earlier, so it was starkly pink and perfect in its small square of ground.

But Luz folded her dress around her anyway, sat down on the fabric-covered crate that served as her garden stool, and began working her hands in the dirt to loosen it. Normally she used a small spade, but today she wanted to feel the dirt, not caring that her clean fingernails would have to be rescrubbed and refiled. It was the way she had embraced earth as a child, back in México, playing in the street-side garden plots. There had been flowers everywhere, and medlar trees dangling their golden clusters of fruit over fences and walls, where street vendors cooked seasoned pork and tacos. There were *catedrales* as old as God, as tall and as silent, and bright *huapango* music coloring the air of the city market. In her memory everyone seemed unworried, their laughter innocent and unafraid.

Mrs. Mulzit appeared next to Luz. "The rose is doing good," she said. "You must have a way."

"My uncle visits us," Luz said, standing quickly and wiping her hands together. "Tonight, he comes for a visit on the way to San Luis Obispo, where my cousins are. One of them who has lost two babies before birth has now just finally birthed a baby."

"Oh," Mrs. Mulzit said. "A baby."

"*Sí*, my uncle lives in Chula Vista and works in a gasoline station," said Luz. "He is all right. He is good."

How easy it was to tell stories! Luz knew no one in Chula Vista, nor in San Luis Obispo, but she knew they were California cities. And Latinos worked everywhere, all over Southern California. Luz amazed herself at her own lies. But they sounded true. They could be true, for someone, somewhere.

"Is it all right for you?" Luz asked.

Mrs. Mulzit seemed to look past Luz, at something else that did not include Luz or the blaring sunlight around them or the cars roaring by on the freeway.

"It is all right," Mrs. Mulzit said finally. Her wide blue eyes caught Luz in a shrewd focus. "This cousin of yours with a new baby, is she a small woman? Small hips?" Mrs. Mulzit pressed her hands on her own narrow hips and flat belly.

"*Sí*," said Luz, her story swirling away from her. "She is not even so big as you," she said to Mrs. Mulzit, who was shorter than Luz by several inches. "She is like a boy, she is so slim."

"*Ja*, now see," Mrs. Mulzit said. "This happens to small women. You tell her to not work so hard when she wants the next baby. I finally got my Willie, my boy in college now, when I rested." She began to laugh, hard. "Though Johanni my husband, he thinks"—she stopped for breath—"he thinks I'm bad luck now, is that not something?"

"Yes, you are right," she said to Mrs. Mulzit, though it didn't seem like the correct response. She fluttered her hands, wishing the grit would disappear from under her fingernails. "Forgive me, I must wash and begin the supper," she said, backing away from Mrs. Mulzit. "This uncle, he comes soon."

"*Ja*, sure, you better get busy, then," Mrs. Mulzit said. She walked down the driveway to get their afternoon paper.

Had Luz's lies brought forth some kind of truth? Did Mrs. Mulzit once lose a baby of her own? Luz hadn't thought that people with so much as the Mulzits, with their fine big house and all the things anyone might want, would ever suffer loss, but of course that was silly thinking. Everyone suffered. But they were the first white Americans Luz had got to know, and they, like her adopted country, seemed invincible. Yet Mrs. Mulzit's old shoes clacked on the driveway, and when she bent down to retrieve the paper, Luz could see the stiffness of advancing age slow her reaching.

Luz wiped her hands on her apron. She had been wearing it with such foolish care. As Mrs. Mulzit came back down the driveway and went past the gate to Luz's little garden, Luz felt her height over the older woman. "Can you say to me, please," she said to Mrs. Mulzit, "why is it that your paper comes now, late in the day? Our paper comes in the morning."

"Yah, sure, ours is the German paper. We come from Austria, you know." She held the paper out for Luz's inspection, though its banner bore words that had no meaning: *Kalifornische Staatszeitung.* "It has more of the news in it than the big one," she said. "That big one has nothing but pictures and selling pages."

Luz stared at the German words, and then at Mrs. Mulzit. She had read about Austria while in school: a place where the people were blonde, the weather cold. There were also Spanish-language newspapers in Los Angeles. Luz had peeked at them in the grocery store. But she made herself read the English paper. Americans read English—do they not? Yet here were the Mulzits, reading a German-language newspaper! Luz felt unsteady on the ground, as though she had just discovered that teachers broke rules, or that priests who spoke of morality were themselves immoral. But such things could happen, and did. Be not such a child, Luz thought to herself. She tried to quiet her thoughts by focusing on Mrs. Mulzit's face, though Luz found the pretty wide-set blue eyes and pale forehead dull-witted, almost bovine.

At that moment Mr. Mulzit drove his El Camino into the driveway, and Diego climbed out of his boss's station wagon at the curb. Luz and Mrs. Mulzit were standing within a few feet of the Mulzits' back door, toward which Mr. Mulzit strode in his characteristic hurry at the same time Diego reached Luz's side.

"Poppa, they will have visitors," Mrs. Mulzit said. "They have an uncle coming to visit. Is that not in the lease they have, that they can have visitors?"

Mr. Mulzit had the darkest eyes of anyone Luz had ever seen—even darker than those of the natives in México. He could have been a wiry Mayan warrior, the kind painted in legends—he was so tanned and compact and alert. But he was a white American; he was from Austria, where everyone was blond, even though he was not blond and never had been.

"Sure, now, sure," he said. "So long as he got papers, just like you guys. Right? When he come, you bring him by and show me his papers, and he can stay a couple of days. Okay?"

Diego shifted from one foot to the other, but did not speak or look up. They all waited for Diego, for him to say, *"Sí,* of course, we will comply with you complete," the way he always graciously deferred to the Mulzits, to their rules, to all things difficult and strange that he and Luz encountered. But he said nothing, though the pulse of muscles in his jaw told Luz that strong feeling trembled there. Perhaps he found he could not lie after all. Maybe it was just that a Mexican man would not have to ask permission to have guests in his own household.

"Well?" Mr. Mulzit said. "Not okay?"

Still Diego did not reply.

"You know, I hear about these uncles," Mr. Mulzit said. He stepped back from Diego, folded his arms, and set his feet further apart. "I seen this before. I'll bet he's some wetback on his way somewhere, and you put him up for the night." He gestured at Diego, as if inviting him nearer. "They pay you?" Mr. Mulzit went on. "They pay you good? I hear it's pretty good pay. I hope it's real good, because you'll need it when you're out in the street again looking for some other place to live."

Diego simply stood there, eyes downcast, as if waiting for a fearsome wind to stop flinging its angry dust in his face.

Mr. Mulzit waited, too, then shook his head, turning toward the stairs. "You Mexicans think you can come and go so when you feel like it," he said. "Look now, you two are okay—don't make trouble for yourself."

Luz touched Mr. Mulzit's arm as he mounted the first stair. "Please," she said, looking up at him, "can you say to me, please?" She swallowed. She did not look at her hand where it touched him. Nor did he. But her fingers seemed to blister there on his skin. "You are a visitor from Austria, yes?"

"Ah, hell, little girl, don't bother me," he said, though he did not shake off her hand. "I came here, and got to be American. I took those tests. I worked hard. That's the way."

"This uncle, his name is Reynaldo. He works hard." Luz's voice sounded strange in her ears. "He has the big family, in California, in the cities with Spanish names, you see. He comes here, like you, and he turns American, like you. *Claro,* he is with papers but he has been here so long, he is not traveling with them, you see." Luz's hand on Mr. Mulzit began to sweat, and he slipped his arm away. "Do you have the papers when you go about? It would be pesty to keep them by, yes?"

Diego went into motion, coming up behind Luz, putting his hands on her shoulders. "My wife, she speaks too freely—please forgive her." He rubbed Luz's neck as he spoke. "We wish your permission to have a visitor, an uncle, for one night only, someone who will not trouble. I myself will certainty his goodness. It is a small thing only."

Mr. Mulzit laughed without smiling. "You are some kind of fresh girl," he said to Luz. "I didn't think your English had got so good already." He jerked his gaze toward Diego. "But how I know he's not some wetback? I run a clean house here, I don't fool with no—"

"We tell to you," Luz interrupted. "It is how you know things. One person telling to another."

"Luz means that you have our word," Diego said, though that wasn't what Luz meant at all. She was looking at Mrs. Mulzit and her small hips, thinking about the slim, boyish cousin that Luz did not have, the babies that were never lost because there was no cousin to have them.

Mr. Mulzit folded his arms. "I don't mean disrespect, but there were some Mexicans next door one time, and they couldn't speak English, but they could say, '*Ja*, sure, *ja*, we legal,' and all that. It turned out they were illegal, and the Immigration guys took them away. And I think it's this Mexican language—if they get the English, it's not so bad—"

"We give you English word," Luz said. She cupped one hand as if an invisible word hovered there. She did not quite understand this practice of giving word, but she knew that the only words that would ever matter would be the ones of America, the click and bite of English, sometimes flickering with meaning and sometimes not.

"Listen, up until a couple months ago you didn't know nothing but Mexican! You barely got enough words yourself to blow your nose, how you give any away?"

"We give you English word!"

"Hell, you don't even know what you're talking about."

"You—you read the German paper!"

"That's none of your damn business." His voice sounded tight, cramped into some smaller space. "You leave our paper alone."

Mrs. Mulzit fanned him with the *Kalifornische Staatszeitung*. "Poppa, I show it to her. She ask, why we get such paper in the afternoon and I say—"

"Ah, you shut up!" Mr. Mulzit flung a sharp wave at his wife. "And you guys," he said to Diego and Luz, "you guys give me trouble, smartalecking around, looking through my newspapers, bringing wetbacks through here like it's some kind of bus station, maybe I forget to renew your lease, huh? You like that?" His wide eyes and red face reminded Luz of her old *abuela*, furious at everything, especially her own oldness.

"We do pray that nothing such as that comes necessary," said Diego.

Mr. Mulzit snapped open his back door. "You do well to pray a little," he said. "Pray that this wife of yours learn to shut up sometimes." The door banged behind him.

Mrs. Mulzit started to follow her husband inside, then stopped. "A man," she said to Luz, and then, "a husband." But her mouth collapsed on the rest of the sentence. "Be careful to keep things in the rooms clean," Mrs. Mulzit said at last, opening the door for herself and disappearing inside.

"*Sí,* thank you, Mrs. Mulzit," said Diego, nodding. "Thank you very much." He put his arm around Luz and turned her toward their apartment, holding her to him tightly. It seemed a long way back, across the broad driveway, beneath the glittering sunshine. Luz felt the strength of Diego's arm around her and wondered if he was angry with her. She wondered if she were angry with him. There would be times again, she knew now, when she would have to speak out for her husband in the world. It was one thing for a wife to make her husband talk to her, but it was another to be his voice with others. Her hands still glowed with sweat. Her heart beat all around her chest as if it had gotten loose. Still, she had spoken, and God had not struck her dead.

When they reached their door, Diego turned to her and took her hands, bent to kiss them, and stopped. "Your hands, *amada,*" he said. He cradled them, wiping at the dirt smudges on her knuckles. "Look at your hands."

It was her turn to be speechless. She pulled her hands away from him and washed them in the kitchen sink. It seemed it was the earth of Guadalajara, not that of a Los Angeles backyard, that flowed down the drain as she washed, as well as something of herself, who had never before this day talked so to a man, nor told a lie. Now the day was full of lies and sharp words. She felt a thin nausea as she remembered her words to Mr. Mulzit. *You are a visitor . . . cities with Spanish names . . . do you have the papers when you go about?* How saucy she had been—how insolent! She kept hearing the words, better than any English lesson ever taught her. But somehow it had become true that this *tío* Reynaldo, whom she did not know, was now hers to defend, worth telling lies for.

Cesar's uncle came after dark, and left before dawn. He was a thin man in his forties, very brown-skinned, with Indian features. He wore two sets of clothes—two pairs of trousers, two shirts, two pairs of socks—all the clothing he would have with him for the summer working in the San Joaquin Valley. He shook his head to offers of food, though he drank glass after glass of water, looking around the room as if gauging its sincerity. Then he smiled at Luz, reached into his pocket and drew out a little packaged Mexican sweetcake, the expensive kind she had often clamored for as a small girl. "Something of México, for a pretty *Americana*" he said in thick Spanish, handing it to her.

Luz took it and smiled back, though she did not open it. *Americana.* Instead of putting it with the other sweet snacks in the cupboard for she and Diego to share, the next day Luz lay the packaged cake in her wood jewelry chest, given her by her mother. It was full of old things: a baby photo of Luz, a photo of her mother at first Communion, a child's necklace with four tiny real pearls, attractive stones gathered from open places around Guadalajara. She wanted the cake to stay sweet and whole inside its plastic, to last as long as baby jewelry and pieces of pink quartz. But after she closed the lid, she thought the chest odd—how like a coffin it looked.

Part II
Exits

4 Vaguely Spanish

As a child, I would sleepwalk. Come morning, you would find me on neighbors' doorsteps. A miracle—a girl curled, her nightgown around her a floral drape. But no one remembered from one night to the next that it was me there sleeping, so the police were always called. It was Southern California, warm at night. Everything smelled like sage. Or manzanita. I can't recall if manzanita has much of a smell. It is merely a pleasant word to say, and sounds vaguely Spanish, like much in Los Angeles. But it wasn't always sage, that much I know. I just couldn't remember the names of fragrant plants.

I had forgotten that I used to sleepwalk until I grew big, put my elderly parents in a nursing home, and bought a small house down the street from where I had grown up. The street was lined with rubbery jade hedges and hibiscus bushes nursed by Mexican gardeners with the blankest faces. A family lived nearby named Ramirez, whose father had tried to kill himself with Valium. This is hard to do, since they make Valium suicide-resistant.

The Ramirezes weren't there anymore. But a family lived in their house who resembled them exactly, down to the two children, an older boy, and a younger girl. When I was a child sleepwalker, the boy used to come into our driveway during the day and beat the shit out of me. He would trap my head in the crook of his elbow and punch my head, over and over. He knew enough to stay away from my face, where bruises appear, inconvenient.

Later, when we were in high school, the boy (named Sal after his father) was courtly, even asked me to a Friday night dance. He was two inches shorter than me and had never had a girlfriend. Later he would marry a divorced woman, and his father would disown him. I said no to the Friday night dance with Sal Junior, telling him instead something girlish and cruel, which I can't remember.

When I finished directing the movers, I went to the old Ramirez house. "Hello," I said to the boy, so like little Sal, who once beat me up at a dance he took me to. Everyone had stood there, not knowing what to do. "You are so like someone I knew who lived here, I just can't tell you."

"Who?" said the boy. "WE live here now."

"The Ramirezes," I said. "They're all far away."

A mother's head appeared above the boy. So like Cynthia Ramirez, heavy, so pale-skinned you'd have thought she was ill. Blue eyes. Very unlike big Sal, her swarthy husband. He had been in Valium in the old days, a sales distributor, and then a respected regional manager.

"Thank you, no," she said.

"I had ham hocks and lima beans in this house once," I said. There was a floral nightgown balled up in a corner by the front door. I pointed. "Someone slept here?"

"A rag," said the mother. "Now, you will excuse us."

*

I had been excused from gym class when I had my period, because I would faint and throw up. Mr. Sal, the sadistic gym teacher for all the seventh grade, would smirk at my excuse when I brought it from the school nurse. I became adept at a cold stare.

We played outside year round, except on bad smog days. Other kids said, if you slept outside at night after the bad smog days, the smog would ball up and suffocate you as it fell down inside the dew. I was afraid and never went outside at night. The world smelled like smoke, like engines burning.

*

You never remembered your own phone number. You forgot keys, medicine, tampons, cervical caps, library book due dates, meetings, things ready at the cleaners, pets' supper times, bills, anniversaries, doctors' appointments for pesky ailments. Where the orange juice jar is. Mothers' birthdays. Calculus equations. Auto registration renewal. The list is perilous.

*

The year I put my parents in their plush nursing home, I kept getting lost whenever I drove there. There are many freeways in Los Angeles—this is something no one forgets, like how the ocean is blue. I would have to take one freeway going south, then another going west, and then still another a brief mile north. You got the endless impression of swirl there, in that home. My parents were content. They did not recognize each other, and occupied separate rooms. My mother sewed, even when there was nothing in her hands. My father happily broke things if left unattended.

It was one of their birthdays, but I couldn't remember whose. I was embarrassed to ask the floor nurses—I should know my own parents' birthdays, after all. So I went from my mother to my father, trying to tell who looked more like the year had changed. All the old people were drinking punch, festive without knowing why. I gave the candy I brought to a man I hadn't seen before, who sat studying the backs of his hands.

*

I rode a neighbor's horse in the sleepwalking days, named Panchita, a brown-black with white flecks at her heels. She was the offspring of some famous Spanish stud in old Palos Verdes when it was really a ranch. She was thirty years old, superannuated for a horse. I was permitted to ride her in her large corral and take her into the orange orchards to graze. In the orchards, I lay on her back while she chewed, and I picked and sucked dry the overripe oranges neglected by the owners. I fell in love with the Mexican gardeners, the one with the blankest face. He was perhaps forty-five, I, a mere eight. I dreamed of sleeping with him in the sage that was everywhere, my eight-year-old love only getting as far as a tender head on his shoulder. Sage was the only plant growing in all of Southern California at that time. Botanists marveled about it in their scientific journals. After a while, inexplicably, other plants returned.

*

My mother was named Sally, though, unbidden, people called her Sal for short. She was a kind mother, dutiful in all the important ways, though on severe occasions she beat me with a pot. In Los Angeles, in the summertime, the brown air becomes a mood unto itself, an especial menace. No one could help themselves. The pot went ping, pock on my legs and buttocks. I screamed, not from the indignity of being smacked as former children say in stories you read. I screamed because it hurt like hell, because my mother was efficient at swinging the pot just so.

*

The Ramirezes beat their sheets with brooms of sage to make them smell like the grand outdoors. The little Ramirez girl had a room all done in pink. You could see Mother Ramirez beating the pink sheets on the line on wash day. The sun shines on the average 352 days a year in Los Angeles. Most wash days are thus safe outside.

*

Every year there is a fiesta in town. There is a parade, in which Mexican-style dancers embrace and whirl their way down the street. Also: Mexican food for everyone, and the mayor riding like a Mexican king in a cab drawn by twitchy Paso Fino geldings. No one in town is Mexican or even vaguely Spanish. Small brown boys, imported from neighboring grade schools where the Mexican people live, beat tiny drums with plastic maracas. They shuffle as though sleepwalking, as though to their deaths. The white people sing & shake their maracas.

*

I begin wearing floral nightgowns again. During the day they are so comfortable. No one caresses my back at night, and no one calls me home for dinner. But I sniff at the air like a naked dog, noting the overripe-luscious sway in the wind. I bring odd flowers to the orange horse-shaped pots people put at the ends of their driveways. My parents puzzled over the horse-pots I brought them, painted with salamanders on the side, but my father performed the act of love that everyone kept forgetting he was so fond of: he smashed the pot with a steel bedpan while laughing in pleasure. My mother, Sal, made her pot her own: she bent her ass over it and crapped in it long and thunderously.

*

My job in office work had been forgettable and productive. I filed things for years, and then told other people how to file and where. For this I was paid thousands of dollars. The men needing the files were lawyers—all had blue eyes, and I kept thinking I'd seen them before. Late at night, when I finished the undone filing from the difficult day, some of the men roamed the halls like sleepwalkers, nodding to me before falling unconscious on the camp cots they kept under their desks. Many pots of Spanish moss adorned their spacious offices, the kind so lush it danced in the stream of the office's mighty ventilation system. I fell in love with a lawyer, who slept with me on his narrow cot, though his body was smoky from hours of cigarettes and bony with long neglect. "Don't forget yourself," he said afterward. He was still the lawyer who beat hell out of cases, I still the keeper of office palimpsests.

*

My parents grew fat. My father in the nursing home required attendants to prevent him from smashing himself and laughing. My mother braided the cords of the window shades together. They don't remember how naughty I was sleepwalking, as long as I buy my mother floral nightgowns. When I present them, she coos. "Touch me there," she says, rubbing herself.

*

Oh, yes. It's a home, but there are bars everywhere. They tell me, no it's not a mental institution. It's safety lock-up, for the forgetting disease, Alzheimer's disease, that eats at mothers and fathers and old presidents alike. I finally remember this when someone with a vaguely Spanish accent writes this down. And then people say, nodding sagely, Ah, Alzheimer's—what a pity. Then, the other things are easy to forget, and the package of meaning they give you with a diagnosis is like comfort, or the relief of moving on to something else.

*

What I don't remember would fill an encyclopedia. There was a little girl who rode a Palomino horse with me. She kissed me at the ends of the days, leaving a vaguely floral scent on my cheek that I'd forget how I got on me. What we called washes used to angle down from mountainsides, but the water's gone and the washes now appear only on maps. The parade organizers have to reread all the parade plans from year to year, because they can't remember the Spanish history of the town that really isn't theirs. They do like the pretty prancing horses and the swirly dancing dresses, so each year there are more of those, and fewer of brown people and ghosts.

I don't remember the day of my birth. I don't remember the screams that split my mother's face when she bore me, or the name of the hospital where she screamed that today is the Church of Scientology of Los Angeles. I don't remember the Spanish conversations the gardeners had, all over the neighborhood during the day, that would waft vaguely on the breeze like the manzanita smell that no one knows. I don't remember the death of the horse I rode in the orange orchard, or her name or what color she was, or what happened after. I don't remember how to use a map—they look like anatomical charts, with horrible red arteries leading everywhere. I don't remember where any of the lawyer files go anymore, or where I put the big goodbye check the lawyers wrote me when I was there the last time. I don't remember who this person is who comes in and cooks my food and keeps me from shredding old books lying around. I don't remember how I get outside at night, or why I discover a different nightgown on myself every evening. I assume Sal Ramirez put these bruises on my head. I don't even vaguely remember why all the Spanish: La Cañada La Crescenta La Loma Gardena Descanso Palos Verdes El Segundo El Monte San Fernando San Marino San Pedro—

3 Florida Postcards

1.

Bungalow houses flake pink paint. Grapefruit and orange trees shit their fruit in a ring on the ground beneath them. The edge of the blue sky has a burnished brown color. And old white couples drive long cars with their windows rolled up. Out of their cars, the men have tiny gray moustaches and spongy noses, and their tanned, bony legs stick out of white shorts. The women have flat butts inside light tailored slacks. But then there are the locals—men with ponytails, women in crop-tops smoking cigarettes—who serve the old people in stores and in restaurants. Children seem invisible, part of the sunlight. Alligators lie on hot asphalt to warm their cold blood, their backs resembling the slung-off retreads that semis leave on the highways. There are fish, and people always in boats.

We had a meal in a restaurant. I ate fish salad off a blue plate. My husband was there, and his eighty-four-year-old mother. He ate a shrimp sandwich, and she had crab cakes, fried brown into disks. Everyone around us was older and white, except for the man seating people, who was Black. He brought me a glass of wine. As we finished eating our food, a woman came out of the kitchen. She leaned on the empty chair at our table. "You seem like sympathetic people," she said. Her hair was blonde, pulled into a tight bun. "Can I sit here?"

"Sure," I said. She sat and put her head down on her folded hands. My husband and mother-in-law and I looked at each other. As we sat there, a man came from the kitchen after the woman. Without acknowledging us, he patted her shoulder and bent to whisper in her ear. As her arms fell to her sides, her face pressed into the placemat. When she slid to the floor, the man gathered her up and took her to the fresh seafood case by the restaurant's front door. He laid her on the case's silver top, her head near the meat scale.

My mother-in-law began to cry. Two boys came in from outside and rifled through the open cash register. The Black man brought me another glass of wine. We left the restaurant amid the confusion, leaving two twenties on the table. I took the full glass of wine with me, drinking and spilling it as we drove.

On the way home in the car, my mother-in-law died in the back seat. We thought she had gone to sleep, her jaw slack. But she tipped over like a bag of groceries when we arrived home and touched her to help her out of the car. My husband wept, biting one of his knuckles through his tears. As we waited for the ambulance, I went out in the hot yard and picked hibiscus blossoms, which I stuffed into the neck of her dress. The ambulance drivers made no mention of the flowers as they laid her on a stretcher, arranging her stockinged feet side by side.

2.

The heat makes a sound in the air, a thin hiss, a hum, like high-tension wires. Women in tennis outfits think again about trying to conceive, and wonder why it's been so difficult. Their husbands, out on chartered boats, cut themselves on fishhooks, and don't think about women at all, or if they do, the women appear disheveled and out of focus. Contrary to popular belief, old people have sex frequently, though old genital tissue is dry, and the elderly go to drug stores as distant as Fort Myers where no one knows them in order to buy lubricant jelly. This old couple here, for example, with the matching white hats, has had sex three times this week, whereas this younger couple, her with the perfect legs, and him with the chiseled jaw, haven't fucked in many days. How do I know this? The prints of the old couple's hands on each other are everywhere, but the young couple's skin is clean and smooth. You only have to look closely, with your sunglasses on, pretending to see something interesting beyond the object of your stare.

After the ambulance drivers were gone, after my husband had made the phone calls to his children, to his sister and brother, and to a funeral home, we began going through his dead mother's things. This was when we noticed the lubricant jelly. It was a new tube, scarcely used, and we wondered, since her husband died many years earlier. We found a drawer of silk scarves, rows of heeled shoes she never wore, and filmy Florida-pink evening dresses still in their store tissue paper.

We decided to donate the clothing to some needy organization. But in Sarasota we could not find one. Along the harrowing, overdriven length of Route 41, there are bagel shops, clothing stores, restaurants, toy stores, dive shops, shell outlets, Sea-Doo showrooms, and porn havens. The needy do not face the open highway.

So we took the dresses to hang in the mangrove swamp. We rented a canoe and piled the dresses into its bow. By the time we got them all them on board, there was only room for one of us. My husband took up the paddle and climbed into the rear of the canoe, and I pushed him off the muddy shore. "Try to keep the taffeta dry," I called after him. "It'll never be the same if it gets wet." He gave me the most mournful smile as he disappeared. A cronk from a startled heron told me where he'd gone.

3.

She'd asked that some of her ashes be scattered at sea and that some be placed by her late husband. She'd left her endless jewelry to this daughter, to that granddaughter. She'd wanted no funeral. But her magazines kept coming. Appliance repairmen kept their appointments with her, made weeks before. Bills came for clothes not yet worn. And the engine of her freezer sang, its compartments secret with food. We stayed in her apartment for days, living off the frozen dinners and pre-cooked shrimp. Egrets came from the pond to the sliding glass door, and we gave them stale Chex cereal. My husband slept a great deal. My mother-in-law's seabound ashes sat in a bag on the dining room table. I stole from her unassigned jewelry pile a tiny crystal brooch.

The phone rang during one afternoon's indoor gloom, and it was a man offering a deal on a motel room in the Keys. "May we bring some ashes?" I asked.

"Sure—wear anything you want," he said. "Your credit card number will hold your reservation."

We drove south in my mother-in-law's black Cadillac. The sky was vast and gray. There had been sightings of rare birds in the bushes above the canal, but we did not stop. The bag of ashes rested in the back seat like a lunch. My husband called out the names of things we passed. "Kingfisher," he said. "Plastic pail." "Airboat." "Sno-cone."

Into the low forests you couldn't see twenty feet, but there were a hundred kinds of produce to buy at the roadside stands. Mangoes, kiwi, tomatoes, corn, strawberries, plus some things no one has ever heard of: ranasset melon, and pipiqueño, a tuber. We bought one of everything, and handfuls of tomatoes, which the brown-skinned people staffing the stands sacked for us, and we set next to the ashes on the car floor. My husband ate tomatoes like apples, piercing the skin with his teeth and taking drippy bites until the fruit disappeared. I fingered the same kiwi for hours until it bruised soft.

When we arrived in the Keys, a peculiar wind had picked up. No answer to our knock at the motel office door but a small, hand-lettered sign: Be back soon. My husband sat in the car with the door open, holding the bag of ashes. I sat on the top step of the stairway up to the office, my mouth open for the wind to dry. We were there when the sun set, and when the wind gave up and died. By then it was dark, and still no one had come. A washing machine ruled the front yard, along with a pair of rusted oil drums. There were conch shells nailed to the yellow stucco walls.

I put my head down on a straw mat on the stair landing and that way slept. My husband stayed in the car and played the radio softly for a long time.

4.

The constellations were seen emptying into the west horizon. Someone lost in a boat off Cuba went crazy waiting for the sun to rise. And just off the dock's end, something enormous stirred in the dark water. By dawn ten families had left for home, two couples decided on divorce, one child vomited herself dry, and three people were declared dead. The steam off the water told all to the people with their ears to the sand. You see the type around in Florida: wizened, watchful. To look purposeful, they often carry a metal detector that they do not use.

On waking, I went to the water's edge and rinsed my mouth with sea water. My husband followed me and watched, carrying the bag of ashes. The sky and the ocean vied for the loudest blue. "This is as good a place as any," I said, holding my hand out for the bag. He handed it to me and made a little sound, like a peep or a whimper.

I put my bare hand into the bag and squeezed out a handful of the damp, uneven grit. One time, a few years before, my mother-in-law fell and we all worried she'd broken something. I held her old woman's hand, rubbery in its purse of skin, as my husband drove too fast to a hospital. Fragments of her dusted me as I pulled my fistful out of the bag. I threw hard over the water, and then reached back in for a second handful. The waves brought the weightless ashes back to us on the beach.

"Let me," said my husband, a choke in his throat. He stripped to his shorts, took the bag back from me and waded into the water. He swam out so far, the bag between his teeth, that I could scarcely see the dot of his head. Later he told me something brushed his feet and legs, not unfriendly. He tore the bag open under water and did not look down.

5.

Children in the Keys grow up with nightmares about ice cap melt. It is not widely discussed, but the water level around Key beaches has been rising a half an inch a year for the past several. People with sprawling, expensive property on the waterfront build landward additions onto their houses, and doodle ideas for the filling oceanfront rooms on their monogrammed letterhead. We, however, moved when the sea moved, keeping our feet dry. You notice how the muskrats know right away that you're dangerous.

We ate breakfast at a Howard Johnson's, stuffing our pockets with extra food from the brunch bar while the Haitian busboys nodded and looked away. My husband's wet shorts made a print on the wooden bench. The restaurant had in it a contingent of career bikers, men in tight black T-shirts and leather boots, and heavy women with voices full of cigarette smoke.

I said, "Why do you all dress alike?"

One of the men called to another, "Get grease or change."

We went full of food back into the sunshine. The dome of blue sky ached above us, its extravagant sunlight spilling into our eyes and down our throats. Even the dark car burned in the heat, its tinted windows a paltry subterfuge. Later in the day, we left the car and went into a garden of a huge vacant house, overgrown with bougainvillea and beach pea. There was some small shade, and a luscious green birdbath with clear water. I could not help myself. I took the bath from its pedestal and set it on the patio, where I stretched myself out and put my face deep in its bowl. The water tasted sharp and greasy. My husband sat down next to me and waited. Finally he removed and tossed his wedding ring in the bowl. "For luck," he said. I retrieved the ring with my lips, proffering it for him to take back.

6.

We lived on the beach for a time. I cut my own hair short without a mirror. We washed in the beach showers before it got light each morning, and ate in raw bars where they don't mind what you wear. That about covers it—what people eat, where they sleep, how they keep from smelling. You probably always want to know that. Otherwise you wonder, you fidget.

We found dead things on the beach: a sea bass about three feet long, its scales like dimes. An osprey tugged out its insides. There was a catfish of some kind, which a determined dog kept trying to eat in spite of the invisible spines. And then there was the gull, a young ring-billed gull, sprawled in a thicket of sea oats. It wasn't dead, and at first I thought it was tangled in fishing line, or in some trap. I picked it up, folding in its wings. It was as light as something already dead.

"It's sick," my husband said, and so it was. Its head lolled as though queasy from all the wind, from the air in its own bones. I set it back down again. "You'd probably better wash your hands," my husband said, and I went to the water's edge. But the stormy gray sky and green water met on the horizon in a stern line, like the firm lips of people who tolerate no nonsense. I was careful, washing in the teeth of the waves. My hands? Growing colder the cleaner I got them.

7.

Fortunately it's warm now, for our clothes are growing thin. We walk like the ever-present egrets around strip malls and watch people eat, notice the colorful stores where they buy clothes. At night I keep hearing someone calling from the shore, but my husband won't let me investigate. He says the water at night is like a bed, whose occupants you don't disturb.

But we found the Cadillac again, and when I sat in it, my head pounded. I held my head between my hands while we drove it to the docks, to a place where boats hang in chambers a hundred feet above the ground.

"That one," I said, pointing to a deep, white boat with a red stripe on the side. Screeching engines got the boat down for us, set it in the water the way you'd turn loose a duckling. The man processing our trade-in of the Cadillac had tiny eyes in a red face and might have been unattractive to me had I bathed indoors more recently.

The boat is anchored down by our dunes, where we sleep in the sea oats every night, where the ring-billed gull finally died into a feathered heap and the ashy fluff of its body powdered into breeze. The boat has enough gas for a thousand miles, to Cuba and beyond. My husband collects provisions during the days. Cans of corn accumulate, and dried peaches and nuts.

At night we talk in the dark about where we'll go, about how we'll put our faces underwater and read the shafts of light if we lose our way. It's coming soon, the night to go, when we'll ruffle into the ocean bed. Florida does not come to an end the way other places do. There is no cliff, no final reckoning place. Instead the grass and land sink away, ditch into salt marsh, go the way extinction goes—with a look back, a little regret, but finally for good when no one's looking. You go in up to your knees, then cringe when your crotch gets wet. Then there's the point where all of you becomes weightless, the way you would float after you're drowned.

I think it's tonight, this dismal, adhesive summer night. We see a light flashing way out. Back when everyone knew Morse code, you might have seen a message in it. But it's just a light somewhere, on a freighter, on a buoy. I try not to be sentimental, for there soon won't be time for it, nor space on the boat. My husband says you stop hearing in the same way after days at sea. He heard this on a talk show once, he says, and then doesn't understand my laughter. I could go without him, by myself, how all women seem to end up. I imagine him drifting away after I've pushed him, his frightened eyes as I wave goodbye.

But you're going to be alone after you're dead, so you take what company you can. My husband's hands have grown rough from his seawater baths, and I want to see what happens to them. I wonder how his cuticles will turn out. Of course, there's more to it, but we plan to leave the weight of detail on shore. You won't hear from us, after that.

6   The Door in the Woods

The cancer did not so much kill Frieda's mother as engulf her like rising water. Within a week of her death, Frieda's father had locked himself in the cabin at the edge of Frieda's property. He had the clothes on his back and the few amenities already in the cabin: a tuberculosis cure cot with raising back, a quilt, a door skin on cinder blocks for a desk. A chair, a functional woodstove, and a spring-fed spigot outside.

John Prade was seventy-eight. Despite the Prades' fractious marriage, their neighbors in Pittsburgh stood ready with casseroles and good cheer after the funeral. He fended off all generosities and phoned Frieda to come gather her mother's things. She drove down from her house on retired farmland in the Adirondacks.

"I want to get the hell out of here," he said when she arrived.

The house had convulsed into unprecedented clutter, as though a huge hand had shaken everything off its shelves and out of drawers.

"Come live with me." Frieda had not planned to say it. "My house is big enough."

"Hell, no. I've seen it. Odd little box of a place. Too much land. Too cold up there. Here there's a furnished apartment across town."

"Let's pack you up today," Frieda said. Where had she acquired such calm? Neither parent had had any to spare. "I'll hire someone to clean this up and ship us the good stuff. Ralph and Cathy can help."

There would be a fight, of course. Days of cajoling, colluding with her brother, Ralph, on strategy. John Prade had the furious visage of a demonic Chinese mask. "You always got your way, didn't you?"

Frieda suddenly thought of her mother, pinched and dying, but strong enough in the last eight days of her life to banish her husband from her sickroom, pointing the way out with a waxy finger. At the time, Frieda imagined this act a kindness, though, in retrospect, there was nothing kind about her mother's fevered eyes.

"Well, I got a blue dress one time," she said. "I remember promising everything for it."

*

Frieda's house was fifteen years old, modest but solid. Large windows brought her to a startling intimacy with firs, white pines, poplar, beech, maple. Her forty acres of browning autumnal grasses opened west toward the tower of Whiteface Mountain like an invitation.

Frieda had moved up from Pittsburgh after Lane, her husband of twenty years, fell in love with a student in one of the Spanish night classes he taught—a woman older than Frieda by ten years, with patrician cheekbones and gleaming silver-blonde hair. They now lived in Utah. The whole of it had crept up on Frieda, who had felt the waning of Lane's attention; fielded the calls from Stephanie, always so very cordial; and finally, marked the passion for stargazing Lane had evolved out of nowhere, requiring late nights out and the purchase of a new telescope whose case never seemed to scuff. The stars above her house on the farmland, so far away from where she and Lane had lived, shone in virulent profusion on cloudless nights.

"I understand wanting to get away," Frieda ventured the second night, serving her father pea soup with lamb. He ate steadily, pausing for a swallow of his beer. "Coming up here was good for me. I can edit medical textbooks anywhere."

She regretted this last admission. Her father seldom passed up an opportunity to berate her for dropping out of medical school in when she was twenty-four.

John Prade finished his soup. "I was wondering about that cabin out there." He jerked his head toward the south window, beyond which the rough one-room cabin stood a quarter of a mile away. Frieda guessed that it had been thrown together as a hunting cabin in the late nineteenth century. "Show it to me."

"Dad, it's night. How about tomorrow?" Frieda said. "It's pretty primitive. Rusted farm junk out there next to it. Broken old bottles."

"Miss Frieda, you have been good to bring me here." John Prade put his elbows on the table and rested his chin on his folded hands. He'd not called her Miss Frieda since she was small enough to be wrestled into the itchy crinoline dresses thought cute for little girls in the early 1960s. "But I don't think it too much skin off your nose to take me out there right now," he continued. " Or I'll find my way by myself."

Frieda stood and busied herself with collecting their dishes and tipping them into the sink.

"All right, I'll take you out there," Frieda said. She tried out a note of exasperation.

He snorted. "Don't do me any favors, girl." But after a long time in the bathroom, John Prade appeared at the back door with his coat on, shod in an abused pair of Wellingtons. Frieda readied her biggest flashlight and led them through the field.

Inside the cabin, he squinted at the sooty ceiling joists and walls as if they caused him pain. When he said he wanted to look things over, Frieda left him the flashlight and returned to the house with only the smoke of the Milky Way for guidance. It wasn't until midnight, while dozing in an overstuffed chair waiting for him, that Frieda began to worry.

She sweated inside the heavy coat she'd worn as she walked back down the thin path in the grass with a small Maglite. "Dad?" she called as she approached the cabin. All the drapes were drawn, but the door window had no cover. The door was locked, and she had no key. She hadn't known the door could lock. "Dad—are you in there?"

She shone the flashlight inside. At first the window threw the beam back into her own face. Then she could make out the recliner, the dead cluster flies and ladybugs piled in the corners, the edge of the cure cot. She shifted the light toward the cot and leaned her cheek against a windowpane. John Prade sat on the end of the cot, eyes on her. He blinked when the light struck his face. Frieda knocked on the glass. "Dad? It's after midnight. Are you all right?"

Without answering, John Prade bent down and pulled off his battered Wellingtons. He drew back the bedclothes and arranged his lean frame on the narrow cure cot, pulling the comforter up to his neck. Once he stilled, only the contours of his body under the comforter marked anything different about the cold disuse of the room.

"Dad?" Frieda knocked once more. "I'm leaving my coat on the doorknob. I'll be back in the morning." A sensible person might have smashed open the door window, broken the lock. Frieda turned away coatless toward her house with inexplicable contentment.

*

Frieda's older brother was a lawyer in Philadelphia. With two reasonable teenaged children and his nice wife, Cathy, Ralph's life had the well-crafted appearance of a Christmas crèche. He was happy, as he always told Frieda, because he had decided to be happy. Frieda found this willed happiness a human miracle, like a great gift for athletics or music.

Ralph approved of their father's move as a temporary measure. "He's still upset about Mom's death, of course," he told Frieda over the phone. "It's so new, even though we knew it was coming."

John Prade had been in the cabin a week. Each night when Ralph asked after him, Frieda said, *I think he's okay*, which was the truth. "Ralph, have you ever wanted to get away from home? Just up and leave it all behind?"

"Of course not," Ralph said. "But I'm lucky, you see. And I work at keeping it that way."

"Well, what if you did? How would you get away?"

Ralph pushed out a breath. "What do you mean? I just said I never have."

The bare birches and white pines that grew along her land's rivulets shouldered each other irritably in the wind. Frieda turned away from the window, took a fresh tight grip on the phone. "Dad's locked himself in my old hunter's cabin."

"He's done *what?*" Ralph bellowed. "How is he surviving out there? It's December now, for Pete's sake! Won't that spigot freeze up? What's he supposed to do for water then?"

"I've been taking food out and putting it on the doorstep." Frieda said. "I take out blankets, and batteries for the flashlight. I got some clothes from the Catholic thrift store in Ausable Forks that should fit him. At least they're warm. He has a saw and a shovel and an axe. He's figured out the woodstove. I think he's thawing snow on the stove for wash water."

She could practically hear Ralph shaking his head slowly back and forth, as if at an opposing lawyer's dim client on the witness stand. Frieda had seen him do this—he had cajoled her into watching him argue a case before a jury once when she and Lane were visiting. "Sis, you said you were reeling him back into civilization."

"He's keeping the place neat, I think." Frieda tugged hard on the permanent braid she'd recently made of her long tangled hair. "He writes me thank-you notes for the food. He was never a big thanker, you know. You remember how he barked at Mom all the time."

"Well," Ralph's voice rose, "are we talking about the same man? My father was gracious and sociable. Happily married. How do you think I got this way?"

"You? The self-made happy man?"

"Okay. Listen. I'll come up this weekend, knock on the door, and if he won't come out, we'll get someone to get him out. You have a local sheriff, right?"

"Ralph, no. Don't do that—not yet. Let me have some more time with him. I know it sounds idiotic, but I think"—she scrambled for a sentence—"I think I can get him to actually go home if I give him more time—"

"Really? Why?"

"He's making a sculpture," Frieda lied completely. "The sort of lawn ornament thing Mom used to like in her garden. I think it's a memorial for her."

"Well, let me know," Ralph said. "Sounds good, actually."

It was Frieda who began the sculpture, using things from the old household dump outside the cabin door. She explored the dump in the afternoons, when John Prade was inside the cabin, the tang of his woodstove fire the only sign of life. He had fixed a sheet of newspaper to the door window. Out of the cold ground came glass bottles: milk of magnesia bottles in cobalt blue; amber motor oil and Clorox bottles; and Cra-Rock seltzer bottles, in glass as aqua as river ice. Frieda coaxed these lost things and others from the pit with lightly gloved hands. A truck license plate from 1940. An empty jar of Lustre-Creme Hair Dressing. Warped and rusted gears, severed from the machines they had served. She rinsed everything in the tap from the spring and arranged the items in pyramids on the porch, by which, she imagined, someone's mother might have been amused. Her own mother had disliked clutter, however, so her grave had only a low, polished marble marker. After her death, John Prade had vetoed the suggestion that the stone also include his name or space for it.

Frieda let one editing deadline go by a few days while she dug in the dirt. And then another, a week. The medical textbook company liked her—it was all right. She even had benefits. At times she forgot the deadlines, forgot about her father inside the cabin while she dug. She had not knocked after the first night. His thank-you notes, scrawled on scrap paper Frieda brought out from her printer, were left pinched between the doorjamb and the door like a thumb.

"Dad, Ralph called. He wants to come get you out of there."

Frieda had brought a chair out from the house and placed it next to the door, where she sat while scraping her finds from the dump. Below the doorknob a crack in the wood ran parallel to the door's length, and it was near this crack that Frieda put her lips when she spoke. "Ralph always was kind of a meddler, wasn't he? He used to come into my room without knocking."

The snows held off for the first week in December, but the television news promised the first storm by week's end. Still the spigot had not frozen. Frieda had bought a new warm coat for herself from the Catholic resale shop. She bought extra-heavy gloves from a mountaineering outfitter in Keene Valley. "I've found a Noxzema jar out here, Dad, in that navy blue glass. With Deco lettering—isn't that from the '30s?" John Prade had been an architect in his working life. His language had been finely rendered angles, his stories the blueprints that bore his name." You always liked that style," Frieda said. "I remember not liking it when I was a kid—it spooked me. It reminded me of the Wizard of Oz."

John Prade didn't answer, but the next day when she went back, the arrangement of tool and bottle she'd been constructing had changed. A rooster weathervane dangled a ringed doorknocker from its cockscomb, both balanced on a feed bucket. A dozen of the bottles snaked nose to tail, no two of the same color touching.

"Dad, one time you asked what was wrong with me that made Lane leave. You said I might be—frigid, and maybe that was my problem." There seemed the tiniest breath coming from the fissure in the door. Flickering stove light—or was she imagining it? "Do you remember how I cried when you said it?"

He had commenced his own excavation in the dump. Fresh dirt piled up beside the pit. He'd hit a mother lode of rusted pest-control items. The "Dead Easy" rattrap; a medieval-looking "Nash Mole Trap," all spikes and collars; and a choker mousetrap, wire guillotines set in a circle atop a square block of wood. These he arranged in a row across the pitted wood of a broken harvester.

A presence manifested on the other side of the crack in the door. Nothing visible, but when she inhaled the space through the door, Frieda thought of how one intuits an object or a silent person nearby in jet dark. She rubbed at a rust stain on a cornflower-blue Bromo-Selzer bottle.

"I used to—sort of—be attracted to other women, Dad." Frieda put down the jar. She scrubbed at a flake of paint on the doorjamb with a chapped fingertip. "Not that I ever did anything about it. But there was a girl in junior high. Her name was Maria. She'd wear dresses out of Qiana, that silky material I've not seen since the '70s. And she was small and skinny. I used to want to take hold of her around the waist. That was it."

A breeze whistled low in the door crack. "I thought about women later, though. When Lane found Stephanie. You know, he had his Spanish class come to the house for a party at the end of the semester that she was in his class. They stayed away from each other the whole party, but I saw him hand her a glass of wine. Then I knew. And then I started thinking about women and their breasts, when I was alone. The more he disappeared, the more I had those thoughts."

A sound like scurrying. A floorboard creak. Then a wedge of folded paper squeezed out from under the door. Frieda retrieved it. Like the other notes John Prade pinched in between the door and its jamb, the triangle of paper unfurled bore only the words, THANK YOU.

*

"You're talking to him." Ralph had that ruffled tone again.

"Yeah."

"And he's not talking back."

"Well, no—except with the notes I told you about." Frieda dug her fingers into her braid. She knew she should undo the braid, wash her hair all the way down. It had been two weeks.

"And this is conversation?"

"Well, he listens," Frieda said. "And I tell him things."

Ralph cleared his throat noisily. All his life, those neglected allergies. Frieda could remember him snoring when she was still sleeping in a crib. "What things?"

"Things I've never told anyone. He doesn't respond, but I know he's listening."

"So." Ralph's voice grew muted. "What have you told him, exactly?"

Occasionally Frieda had gotten the upper hand with her brother during their childhood. Her ability to do so had been like predicting the weather—she could generally tell which situations would turn to her advantage, but nothing was guaranteed. She hadn't sought it much. Ralph seemed to be a good brother. But she felt the same change in the timbre of his question that she'd come to recognize long ago as the shift of power. "I've told him about—my marriage. About Lane. About a girl from school. About you, some."

"What did you tell him," Ralph's big baritone condensed to a whisper. "About me?"

Under the bridge a mile away from Frieda's land the Ausable River furled itself into menacing rapids. Their churn took hold of her and Ralph, as though the craft of their conversation had lost its rudder. "I said you were pushy when we were young. I said you came into my room without knocking."

"Did you tell him what—happened one time ? You know, that time?"

Frieda searched the dark city of her memory. Something had happened. But then, something had always happened. What you did was knuckle your forehead and try to forget. She suddenly felt so, so tired, the way she'd worn out from her own grief when Lane left. "I don't know what you're talking about," she said to the pinprick holes of the phone's mouthpiece.

"You did tell him. About when—I came in. I just wanted to see—a girl. Curiosity used to be healthy. The hairbrush was a really bad idea. You know I said I was sorry."

"Ralph, I didn't—"

"I was only thirteen years old!"

The recollection as ordinary as that of breakfast, or a fishing trip in the summer. Ralph pinning her to the bed, bribing her with promises of candy and niceness, so he could look between her legs and put things up inside her. She'd been nine. "Look, Ralph, how do you think I could tell Dad anything like that? I wouldn't tell anyone that. I never even told Lane."

"I'll bet you're lying. I'll bet you told Dad."

"Oh, go make yourself happy over this one," she said, so weary. "For Christ's sake."

Ralph cleared his throat again, sharp and loud. "I'll come, that's all. I'll come up and explain things to him. I'll get in the car tomorrow. You'll be there, right? Though I guess it doesn't matter if you are or not. I know the way. You've got the key to your house under the stairs on a nail."

"Go to hell, Ralph."

"No joke. I'll be there by dinner tomorrow. Don't say anything to him."

But Frieda had not been joking. "Okay," she said.

Back in 1962, Frieda's mother had discovered Ralph at his investigations of Frieda and punished them both. That was the end of it. "I don't know if you heard about it," Frieda continued to the crack in the cabin door. "We were grounded the same as if we'd been caught stealing, or gotten bad grades at school."

Nothing stirred. The first storm had left five inches of snow. The spigot worked briefly at midday and then froze up again in the afternoon. John Prade had been building fires to warm it; charred logs spiraled out from the spigot's entry point into the ground.

"Dad, he's coming tomorrow to explain things to you. He thinks I told you before now. You—and me, too, I guess—are standing in the way of his happiness. You know how he feels about happiness."

The evening was so still that the tiniest thing moving in the woods resounded like the snap of a leg breaking. It might have been a grouse, or a deer. A red squirrel. "Won't you explain something to me, Dad?" Frieda said. "It doesn't have to be why you're—here in my cabin. It's your cabin now. I mean, how about the theory of stresses in a skyscraper? Is there a formula you can rely on? How do architects know one building will stand and another won't? I never paid attention. I was—looking into the body. Did you know the body is like a building? That's what my anatomy teacher said."

Frieda was about to rest her forehead against the doorjamb when the door opened with a ripping sound. She jerked back and stood up. Inside, the orange lights of a fire pulsed through the slits in the wood-stove door. She waited, frozen on her feet. It had begun to snow. John Prade appeared and motioned her to come in.

The smell of the room was chaotic with extremes: unwashed body and balsam fir. Food beginning to turn, and the thick, sweet odor of hot wax from a few struggling candles. Crushed old newspaper, clothing from the last century, pine needles, mouse and squirrel shit spilled out of a fresh opening in the south wall. Charred drips streaked the flanks of the woodstove, and the floorboards blurred under a new layer of grime.

Her father stood like a stake in the center of the room. His new beard was stone white, his eyes glassy, and his bearing absolutely erect. When he tugged off his black knit cap, as an antique gesture of respect, Frieda supposed, his hair whorled around his head as if wind-whipped. She had not seen him face to face in a month.

"I have in mind my last design," John Prade said. His terrible glance swept the room. "Engineering the end of futurity."

There was no precedent for this moment. The most Frieda had ever directly addressed with her father were calculus problems when she was in high school, and that had not gone well. "That's—well, that's just crazy sounding, Dad."

When he swung his gaze to her, Frieda had to squint, as if at sun thrown off bright metal. "You are not the only one who wants to get away," he said. "I'm just not coming back."

Their eyes were the same color: blue gray. She stared back. It was then that she noticed the liter of vodka on the floor. The locals call vodka in zero temperatures "suicide juice."

"Why?"

"Look at you, sequestered up here like a nun. And why is that? Because you can't abide the smell of your own life. You and that boy-husband. Just try to tell me you'll ever get over it."

Frieda couldn't draw a full breath. "You—you and Mom. What a lie—"

A mirthless smile. "Exactly correct."

"And all those years I thought your disdain a kind of love."

"So you see."

Frieda thought her whole body might fly apart. She felt she could kill and find it good. "So I see WHAT? That you're giving up on life because you made a wreck of it? That you can't do without Mom because she gave you someone to blame for your misery?"

"One side of the arch hates the other and pushes on it like a bull. That keeps the roof up."

"What—you and Mom were a roof?"

"What do you think, Miss Frieda? Did we keep the rain away and your brother out of your drawers?"

Frieda felt the death-chill in odd places: the palms of her hands, inside her elbows, deep inside the curving walls of her hipbones, like cramps from the menstrual periods she'd stopped having over a year before. "I should never have told you that."

A green log in the woodstove hissed as its sap boiled. John Prade considered his black knit cap as he crushed it in his hands. "Only a corroborating detail."

He was on a plane about to crash, alive but doomed. "I don't have a mother anymore," she said. "I'm not ready to give up a father, too."

"I'm sorry for that."

"Don't leave me." It cut Frieda's throat to say it. She'd said it to Lane.

"But I will. Sooner or later. It can't be helped."

Frieda went to her father and put her arms around him. He caught her in his arms like a lover. Never had they hugged so, not at graduation nor wedding day nor funeral. His body was as bony as a tree and smelled of rank, wild things. She loathed tears, but they poured down her face. She released him, and he stepped away.

"I still don't understand," she said, scrubbing her cheeks with a wool glove.

"I think you do." John Prade fetched and drew on another coat— the oversized one Frieda had given him his first night in the cabin— over the three he was already wearing. "You could have turned the dogs loose on me long ago."

"I still can, you know," Frieda said. "I only wanted you to be mine."

John Prade went to the door and opened it. The frigid air poured its leaden weight into the room. "I will be, from out there," he said, pointing at the thickening snowfall and to the blurring trees beyond. "If you'll let it."

Frieda dove into her parka and found her footing on the snowy porch. "I'll get Ralph. I'll get searchers."

But her father had already shut the door behind her.

*

By the time Ralph arrived three hours later, the snow was falling fast. He stooped to kiss his sister but caught himself and drew away after an awkward shoulder squeeze. Without removing his coat, he retightened his scarf and turned up his collar, turning to Frieda. "You know, I'm sorry about that—fooling around back then. Did I ever apologize?"

"No. But never mind about that now," Frieda said. She'd finally washed her hair, which cascaded damp and loose down her back. "It doesn't matter anymore."

Ralph returned in an hour. John Prade was gone. "Could he be somewhere else?" Ralph asked. "Could he be in the house? The garage?" When Frieda shook her head, Ralph threw his arms wide. "No footprints, of course—not with snow falling this hard. You got snowshoes?"

They searched until thwarted by a muddled, gray twilight boiling with snowflakes. Inside the house, they smacked snow off their clothing and kicked it out of their boots. Frieda could see Ralph trembling once he shed his parka. "That place he lived in—did you see it?"

"Yes."

"How did the walls get all charred like that? Somebody must have tried to burn it down. The bed scorched. No furniture. All the walls gutted? The insulation torn out? Did he do that?"

Frieda had avoided a direct glance at the cabin while they were searching, as though it were a former friend encountered on the street whom she'd badly failed. "It was never in the greatest shape," she said.

Ralph found a beer in the refrigerator, one of a six-pack their father had never finished. He downed it quickly. " We need to call rescuers, maybe the sheriff. You got their number?"

The snow had fast laid down a six-inch blanket. In her mind's eye, Frieda watched her father moving through the furred quiet of the snowy woods. He'd be dressed in his tinker's layers, but his topcoat, the one Frieda had left for him his first night, would flap around unbuttoned. He'd have his shovel and his axe. He'd go up into the wildest part of her land, beset with blackberry brambles and willow and infant poplar all struggling for daylight.

Nothing particular would mark the place where he would dig himself the grave that a trespassing dog will discover and bark at for hours the following spring. After taking what must have been days opening a hole in snow and hard ground only a week from freezing, John Prade will lie down in the cold hole, drink the vodka down, & cover himself well with dirt, pulling it down from a pile he'd made weeks before. In the spring, defying her attempts to shoo him away, the dog will hover with unmistakable sorrow as Frieda brushes aside the leaves and dirt enough to behold her father's corpse in its hole, his flesh and clothes merging with loam, before she closes the hole above him again.

This strange dog, black with white question marks over each eye, will always appear when she approaches the grave with a weekly offering of river stone that she will bring in by wheelbarrow through the muddy forest. The dog will mark the swelling cairn with his urine each time, gazing at her regretfully as he holds his leg back like a salute. Covered by duff and stone, his scent masked by dog pee, John Prade will belong to Frieda at last.

All I want to know is where Dad is, Ralph will say one day to the wide, lush field during a visit that summer, drinking gin on her porch. He will have had a full retinue of law enforcement search and fail to find from Lake Champlain to Montreal. As Ralph's wife and teenagers play badminton on the coarse grass, he will look heavenward. Can't I just know where he is?

No, Frieda will think. *No, you may not.* And something like bliss will fill her.

Part III
Return

7 Camarado

She was forty-nine years old, with graying, elbow-length hair thin and pale as dental floss. Both lean and nervous, she and her husband Frederick doted on each other and on a pair of Lhasa Apsos, the dogs' long fur blending with Priscilla's streaming hair as she held them in Christmas photographs. Though the prairie of their fifties and beyond stretched before them, both were well employed, Priscilla at her own upscale Southern California coffee house, Frederick as part-time accountant, part-time waiter at a Mexican restaurant. Along with a few friends, no debt, and careful steerage around trouble, they were as complete as their wedding china, still in its boxes after twenty-five years.

Except Priscilla was pregnant. Frederick had had a vasectomy as soon as the procedure had become more widely available in the 1970s, and Priscilla had been so faithful to Frederick that the word had emptied out of meaning. To her Frederick and the sexual act were as indistinguishable as lungs from breathing. And both of them agreed, Frederick vocally and sometimes harshly, and Priscilla in quieter tones, that there were too many children in the world already. Privately, both realized that any parenting tendencies either had were spent on each other. That, they told themselves, was a good and rare thing.

As rare as a forty-nine-year-old monogamous wife of a sterile man conceiving for the first time. Priscilla had worried that her missing menstrual period warned of imminent menopause, or, worse, disorder and disease. But when the shiny-eyed gynecologist twenty-five years Priscilla's junior presented her the news, Priscilla had shouted out "No!" as though she'd just been asked to vote Republican, or consume meat.

"Yes, I'm afraid, yes," said Dr. Holly, seeming in her pleasure younger than her thirty-four years.

"You're afraid," said Priscilla. "You're not the one with the problem."

Dr. Holly shrugged. "It doesn't have to be a problem. It's not an illness. Unlike the thinking in the old days."

"Frederick had a vasectomy before you graduated from high school."

Dr. Holly's grin increased in wattage. "Nothing's foolproof."

"And I've been faithful, if that's what you're thinking."

"Not at all."

Priscilla let Dr. Holly give her a list of instructions and schedule her for a thorough prenatal care visit the following week. "Unless you're considering—not proceeding." Dr. Holly paused to watch Priscilla's face.

Frederick and Priscilla had been passionate vegetarians since before they had met in their early twenties. Full vegans, in fact, since milk products require cows to be pregnant and thus calves to be slaughtered, and mass egg production compelled appalling care of chickens. Even their two dogs ate only plant-based food, though their vet had to do bloodwork on them regularly to make sure they were healthy. Not living on animal death comforted Priscilla more than she could explain. Fortunately, she didn't have to, since Frederick considered meat eating—and meat eaters— abnormal. Still, they both adhered to pro-choice abortion views, as their friends did, as other lifelong Democrats did, as anyone reasonable should, said Frederick.

"I have to think about all this," Priscilla said.

"Of course," said the doctor, patting Priscilla on the knee. Dr. Holly scribbled on her prescription pad. "Call me—here's my private office number."

Priscilla folded the paper square into her wallet. The doctor left, and Priscilla crumpled her paper gown. Naked, she could see to her feet easily over the mild curve of her belly, no distention evident yet. Perhaps it was a mistake. Unlike other pregnant women she'd known, Priscilla had had no inkling. The new thing inside her had kept quiet. Still, she knew it was true. She'd been attributing a vague, fresh anxiety to the demands of her coffee business, to turning fifty in six months. She'd been watching Frederick more carefully lately, wondering if something ailing him had been signaling to her. But it was the new thing inside her that was signaling, the thing she and Frederick had made.

Priscilla walked home from the doctor's, down the wide boulevard that traversed their hillside suburb, fifteen miles from downtown Los Angeles. They had lived there since their marriage, back when the suburb's most numerous residents were orange trees and avocado orchards. Now SUVs and Mercedeses and Jaguars roared on the boulevard's length and up into multimillion-dollar homes in the hills. Frederick and Priscilla maintained with love their tidy bungalow built after the Second World War, and though their yard boasted flaming birds-of-paradise and lantana and bougainvillea, were they to abandon it, their house would be bought, bulldozed, and replaced within months as had been neighboring houses of the same style and vintage. Priscilla and Frederick let the ivy and the red-berried pyracantha thicken around the borders of their yard, obscuring their views of the redone sidewalks and of the new 10-bedroom Romanesque villa across the street.

Instead of going right inside the house when she arrived, Priscilla went to the bench Frederick built from scrap lumber under their loquat tree, its branches heaped with their sweet yellow fruit. When she sat down, Priscilla's head grazed the freighted branches. It was a hot, bright September day, and under this canopy, Priscilla welcomed the retreat from sun and view. She wondered how it might be to live the life of a stone yard ornament: a Greek maiden pouring water from a jug, a frog, a curled fawn.

Frederick had seen her come home and let out the dogs, who wiggled and flowed around her feet in greeting. He approached from the house and caught up a heavy branch near the bench to admit himself as though lifting a flap to a tent. His long, fierce face with its hawk nose and large dark eyes, framed with licks of hair gone from black to bright silver, struck her as much as it had when she'd met him back in college, when both of them were with groups of friends shooting pool. She had been playing, badly, and he had only sat, glowering, at the foolish activity. She'd been drawn to his brooding energy, to his tendency, even at twenty-two, to set himself apart, to scorch the wanting world with his intense, critical eye.

"How are you?" Frederick said, fondling a cluster of loquats.

"I'm fine," Priscilla replied.

"I mean the doctor's appointment."

"Also fine."

Frederick began picking off the riper fruits, accumulating them into his shirt, which he'd pouched up from the hem to make a pocket. "So nothing's wrong? Just normal menstrual fluctuations?" He stood up and intensified his gathering, moving into the higher laden branches. "I can take these to work tonight. Julio does a sauce with fruit. He'll like these."

"Frederick?" Priscilla spoke from under the branches. She could not see Frederick's face. At her feet the dogs splayed themselves out, greedy for the sun's heat even on the hottest days. "How long have we lived here?"

Frederick peered down at her through the long loquat leaves. "Twenty-seven years, nine months, and I think ten days, baby. You know that, don't you?"

"I guess I haven't kept close track."

She had a glimpse of him smiling through the leaves. "That's why I keep your books for the café and you don't."

"Frederick?" She wished for something to say that could engineer in advance the moment of accommodation. Something wise and patient and completely in control. "I'm pregnant. I found out at the doctor's."

He sank back down on the bench, his lap full of yellow fruit, his lips parted and jaw soft, as if in sleep. His huge, bony hands folded around the pouch of loquats. "You're not joking."

"No."

Frederick dropped his gaze instead to the clusters under his hands. "I don't know how that's possible."

"I don't either, but the doctor said nothing's foolproof."

"You said this doctor was a little young? A little rushed through medical school? They're all in a hurry to get out and start paying off those loans and start living the high life, aren't they?"

"Oh, Frederick, for Christ's sake." Her stomach twitched. "She's not a nitwit and I'm not screwing anyone else and I haven't the faintest idea why this happened. And I know it's not a government conspiracy or aliens or fundamentalist Christians. Apparently vasectomies can pop a leak. Male fish turn female. Spiders travel for miles on their little filament sails." Priscilla began to cry, and because she seldom did, it hurt, searing her eyes and closing her throat.

Frederick let the loquats tumble to the ground and scooted across the bench to her side. "Baby," he said, taking her in his arms and blotting her cheeks with his sleeve. "I'm sorry. Don't worry, I'll take care of everything." He smiled into her face and tucked a fingerful of her flossy hair behind her ear. "Thank heaven abortion's still legal for now, when we really need it."

*

Priscilla was struck with a strange lassitude, which showed itself in clumsiness at the café and inattention at home, as though she were listening to something disturbing just out of range. Frederick took charge of calling Planned Parenthood, scheduling the abortion, and arranging a massage-therapy session for Priscilla the day after. Priscilla continued her routine of rising at five-thirty to open the cafe by six, but found herself startled by the increasing darkness at that hour as the year waned. Everyone looked tired to her. She forgot to pity the young housewives with their diamond rings and their sweatsuits into which they never sweat, as they parked for hours with their lattes and the *Los Angeles Times* in the cafe's corners after their husbands went to work at seven o'clock.

She also kept her prenatal appointment with Dr. Holly, without telling Frederick. "How are you feeling this week?" Dr. Holly said.

"Tired," Priscilla answered, thinking of the predawn customers, especially the men, with their hollow eyes and smell of sleep, despite doses of aftershave. "Really tired."

"That's normal," Dr. Holly said. "You're in very good health, so I expect routine symptoms at this point: the fatigue, nausea, aches, perhaps some insomnia. Still, we should do an amnio in a few weeks because of your age, make sure there aren't any—disorders."

"What then?"

Dr. Holly got a serious look, offering Priscilla a glimpse into her mature face, at the older woman she would be. It would be a soft, mannish face, alert, guileless. "That would be up to you. And your husband. How did he take the news, by the way?"

"Oh, he's full of plans," Priscilla said.

"Glad to hear it," Dr. Holly said. "Looking toward the future—that's good."

*

Frederick and Priscilla walked for exercise, around their neighborhood and up into the foothills, where the pricey homes gave way to a scrubby nature trail lined with chaparral and greasewood. Where they saw hawks and coyotes and mule deer, and from which they could see into Pasadena to the east and Los Angeles and the ocean to the south if the day was very clear. The afternoon following the prenatal care visit, Priscilla took their walk alone, as Frederick had been called in early to the restaurant to cover another waiter's absence. Their usual loop included a stop at the trail's highest point by a power-line tower, huge and gray, its wires seething with electricity. The day Priscilla stopped there alone, pregnant, exhausted, and due at Planned Parenthood in three days for an abortion, she considered the looming tower, holding up its lines so that the lines in Tujunga would hold up, too, as would the ones further west toward Sunland. She said out loud to the tower, looking up its vast legs: "I don't want an abortion. But what should I want instead?"

*

The morning of the abortion, Priscilla awoke early and watched Frederick sleep. She had never withheld from him a single thing she'd felt or done. Now he knew nothing of the prenatal visit she'd kept, of her plea to the power-line tower. But the little thing inside her had divided them. They slept in a double bed, too small, really, for the pair of tall adults they were, but to Priscilla all their nights of sleeping so close had blunted their separateness. Now she was set apart, brooding alone around this strange, fresh simmer. Couples who welcomed children must have more room between them. She and Frederick even wore each other's jeans, so alike were their bodies.

Frederick opened his eyes, focusing on her, as though he'd been just pretending to sleep. "You all right?" he said.

"I've been thinking."

"No wonder about that." He caught the ends of her hair, bright even in the dawn darkness, and wound them into a curl. "If you feel like it later, I'll make you some matzo ball soup." It was Frederick's specialty, tricky for a vegan: sticky white rice instead of crumbs and egg for the balls, and vegetable broth enriched with sesame oil to suggest chicken soup. It was luscious, and he'd fooled more than a few carnivores.

Priscilla sat up and propped her back against the headboard with her pillow. The dogs curled in their baskets by the door, fixing them with identical stares. "I don't want to do this," Priscilla said. "I don't want to go through with it."

"I don't blame you," Frederick said. "But they'll give you painkillers, and remember, the practitioner said you could get a general if you wanted it."

"No," Priscilla said. "I mean, I don't want to kill it. I—can't."

"Baby, the alternatives don't look good."

"I know."

They lay staring ahead for some moments. "Well," Frederick said, "I can't not do it. I can't do the kid thing."

She turned to him. "Why not?"

"This is something I thought we never even had to talk about. There are a hundred reasons why the world can do without another human." His huge eyes flared, their whites glowing in the dim light against the brown irises. "There are another hundred why I can do without being a parent. I couldn't even keep a turtle alive when I was a kid."

"You never told me that," Priscilla said.

He pulled the sheets up around his neck. "Not something I'm exactly proud to tell."

"Hon, you do fine with the dogs. And with me." She could hear herself almost wheedling.

Frederick still had a fierce look. "And that's about as much care as I've got in me." When she ducked her head, he took her in his arms. "Come on, baby—our world's so fine. Why change it? We'd have to buy bright plastic items, a huge stroller, and a minivan. And then there'd be babysitting groups, and soccer, and bad violin practicing. I can't bear it. I've been thinking about grafting that avocado tree—you know? The young one in the back yard? And then we'd have avocados. You think we'd have time and energy and interest for stuff like that if suddenly a kid took us over?"

"Mightn't it—a child—be fun at all?"

Frederick threw off the sheet and got out of bed. The dogs burst into wiggles and ankle licks. "Here," he said, going to the closet and reaching deep inside it. Priscilla switched on the lamp by the bed. "You can wear this today— won't it help?"

Frederick had drawn out her wedding dress, a dusty pink-and-yellow cotton gown that fit as well as the day she'd bought it. She wore it on their anniversaries, and on days when she felt blue. She rose and slipped into the dress, letting him lift it over her head. Inside the dress, she felt no less uneasy about the morning's intentions, but she couldn't say no to Frederick, any more than she could have said no years before, when, with a straighter back, under his seizure of black hair, Frederick had gripped her hands during their vows so hard they bruised.

*

Priscilla took the general anesthetic. She'd never been anesthetized before in her life, so she was unprepared for the groggy irritability that afflicted her all afternoon. She swallowed the Vicodin dispensed by the solemn nurse as they left Planned Parenthood, but the cramps welling up from her stripped interior heeded no palliatives, including the kava tea for relaxation that Frederick made after nothing else helped. She felt like vomiting but didn't, too tired for the necessary strength. The vegetarian matzo ball soup cooled untouched next to her recovery station on the sofa. Frederick tried offering Priscilla her favorite novels, and when she shrugged them away, he went and got *The Poky Little*

Puppy, an original edition saved from her childhood library that she loved. At Priscilla's aghast expression, Frederick put the book away.

Frederick rubbed Priscilla's feet for a long time, the only thing that relieved the aching in her belly and legs. As evening approached and she began to feel better, Priscilla watched Frederick's head bent over his work of manipulating her white feet with a sensation that she hadn't been able to identify through the din of her discomfort. When the misery began to abate she knew, and it shocked her: it was contempt that twisted her mouth at his stringy neck and the elderly bend to his shoulders, features she'd never found odd or unlovable before.

Her foot in his hands twitched and stiffened. He stopped rubbing, but held the foot in his warm hands, not looking at her. "You didn't really want it, did you?" he said. "The—fetus? I read that every woman has misgivings in prospect, but later, when it's all over—"

The tiny specter of contempt jerked back down its hiding place. Instead, just for a moment, a hot red anger flared. "I'm just tired, hon," Priscilla said.

"Baby," Frederick said, too late sucking back the word. "'Cilla," he began instead, with Priscilla's childhood nickname. Again, childhood. Priscilla shut her eyes, hard. Would there no end to the electric brushes against what they'd done?

"It'll just take time," Frederick said, putting into words what Priscilla had been about to say. "All these things take time." As if in mocking answer, someone next door jerked on a gas-powered weedwhacker, farting and sawing. Frederick glared at the window admitting the noise, and Priscilla quailed again at his fierce look, the same as the one he'd given her in bed that morning, when she'd told of her uncertainty. She added this fear to the growing list of other unmentionables: her conversation with the power-line tower, her contempt, her single prenatal doctor's visit. These things she stowed inside and tamped down smooth.

*

For weeks afterward the weather became so soft and perfect Priscilla thought she might be dead. Fall in Los Angeles was usually wildfire time, big wind time, deep unwashed smog time, but not that fall, not those weeks. The days waxed dewy as spring, warm and clear around the noon hours, and freshly cool at dusk.

Frederick grafted the avocado tree and made loquat jam. He lifted his usual ban on the wastefulness of cut flowers and made sure a handful of something bright adorned the kitchen, a single bird-of-paradise, a cluster of naked ladies with their pink trumpets, late giant purple iris. He kept up his rubbing of Priscilla's feet, even though she felt well within a few days. She went back to work and said little to Consuela and Farleigh, her café employees of many years, as timid and anxious to please in their presence as if she were working for them.

The only thing amiss was Priscilla's appetite. She had always enjoyed the vegan matzo ball soup, the vegetarian lasagna, the burdock root and blood oranges and silken tofu that loomed large in their diets, loved them for their inoffensiveness, their simplicity, even for their inconvenience, for until recently these foods required from supermarkets a special order. Priscilla liked that, too, the quiet insistence on their unobtrusive way to live and consume. But the familiar textures and flavors repelled her. Frederick knew her tastes had moods and seasons and so did not mention her muddied but uneaten bowls of soup, the medallions of expensive organic burdock root left undisturbed on her plate.

But then it was Consuela's birthday. Priscilla closed the café for lunch and took Consuela and Farleigh at the Starlight Inn, an old-style, dimly lit, overstuffed-bench chop-house nearby, and Farleigh was buying because he insisted. Priscilla let the two of them go before her to their table, and when a waiter went by with a platter the size of an end table loaded with a huge, smoking steak, a terrible longing rose up in Priscilla like pain. Her last bite of meat had been a casual burger when she was still a young teen. But her body had not forgotten the use of meat, just as it had not forgotten how to conceive, how to scorn, how to kill. As she cut into the same sirloin steak special she'd seen go by, that she ordered for herself without explanation to Consuela and Farleigh, their shocked stares beat like sunlight on her hands and mouth and plate.

The flavor of the animal flesh, like blood from a cut finger, rolled around in her mouth that night as she lay next to Frederick. In the days following, she ate her lunch alone at the Starlight Inn, again and again ordering the sirloin special, and when the special ended, eating thick rare burgers instead. Frederick stopped rubbing her feet, saying curtly that they smelled strangely. When they made love, Priscilla ignored Frederick's furtive nose to her skin under the guise of nuzzled affection.

One day he came up behind her in the kitchen while she was up to her elbows in dishwater. "You smell like someone else," he said, pausing. "You can tell me—is there someone else?"

At this Priscilla drew back from the soapy sinkful with a plate in one hand. She turned to face him, wrists dripping. "No," she said, letting the dish slip to the tile floor, where it sparked into fragments.

They stared at the sudden mess around their feet. "You dropped that on purpose," Frederick said, his bulging eyes glittering.

"Yes."

She could tell he wanted to ask why, but he'd not had to ask her the why of anything in years, so unfolded to him had been all her motives, and his to her. He'd forgotten how to ask why. So he didn't, and Priscilla could tell that he took for an explanation instead the worst of his own fears, that she was lying, that someone else had come between them. He stalked away, leaving her to mop up the glass shards and soapsuds, to bind her finger herself when a piece of shatter she couldn't see cut and made her bleed.

*

Priscilla tired of the Starlight Inn. She found precooked and packaged chicken breasts and barbequed ribs at the gourmet supermarket in town instead, taking the squeaking plastic containers of them to the park near the elementary school on her lunch break. At home she still picked at the vegetable dinners Frederick made, but it shamed her that she felt herself strengthening and gaining alertness as the days of carnivorous eating continued. She felt as though she was reclaiming a foreign language she'd long forsaken for its embarrassing gutturals.

As her daytime meat-eating continued, so did her strange smell, his suspicious watching, their truncated conversations. Priscilla found a few alarming books around their house about uncoupling, surviving divorce, weathering the loss of a love. Frederick took the dogs for walks without asking her if she wanted to go. She read the relationship books. She knew she should do something, take his hand, apologize. She imagined relevant scenarios. But a tight, cold set of gears inside her would not allow her to ease into the small motions necessary. She saw what she should do and could not do it.

*

The rains of winter began in late November. Frederick donned his clear plastic rain suit and tended the grafted avocado tree, which since its graft was not faring well. It had begun to pitch off its leaves, dry out at the branch tips, shrink inside its bark. Priscilla knew that there were a few things the gardener could do to help, involving the adjustment of soil acidity and clever pruning, and that Frederick had already done them. So whatever he was doing out in the rain with the avocado tree went beyond scientific necessity. She watched him from inside the house. He fondled leaves, dug and smoothed over sodden dirt at odd distances, massaged the thinner branches.

With a pang she recognized these ministrations as resembling those he'd given her those weeks before following the abortion, and something about that pang, its timing or its intensity, gave the frozen set of gears within her a wrenching quarter-turn. She whipped her brittle hair into a ponytail so tight her temples stung. She looked around for a rain slicker, and then an umbrella, and then decided she didn't care about getting wet. The dogs cowered in their baskets near the kitchen heat vent as she stomped around the house, going one way and then another.

At last she burst out the back door, the rain pelting into her eyes and scalp, a cold, serious, efficient rain that would bring the flowering mock-orange trees back to life in January. The rain seemed to assault her, to misunderstand her, to not care that she might need something different from what it insisted she have, and the wetter she got as she reached Frederick with his back to her in the garden, the more furious she became. It was not reasonable, she knew. What happened next she would regret. But the creaturely demands announced by her brief pregnancy would not let her deny them again. What she did not choose had left its failing trace. Her body wanted to explode, to shriek, to strike in every direction.

"For your information," she said through the hiss of the rain to Frederick, who gaped up at her in surprise, "I went to the doctor once without telling you because I thought we might want that baby. I yelled about it from a mountaintop. And I've been eating meat and liking it for almost a month. The dogs have been getting the scraps I bring home. Why else do you think they get frantic when I come home now, when all they've ever eaten was textured vegetable protein?"

The rain dripped into Frederick's upturned face from the brim of his plastic hat. The look he wore reminded Priscilla of a stopped clock. They stared at each other for a time in which Priscilla forgot the rain until her eyes filmed over with rivulets down her forehead. Then Frederick contracted his silver-flecked eyebrows into a straight edge. "I wonder if I'd rather you were fucking someone else," he said, low. "Jesus Christ, Priscilla, you might as well be, taking in someone else's flesh—"

She whirled round in her sodden sneakers toward the toolshed across the grass from the tree garden. She grabbed the maul, on hand for the occasional nights cold enough for a wood fire, when Frederick split logs for the fireplace. Normally it was too heavy for Priscilla, but an electric strength animated her thin arms as she strode back to Frederick and the tree. She stood before him hefting the maul, and he backed away. He cried out once at the first swing of the sharp edge into the avocado trunk, only as thick around as a piano leg. And then he was silent as she swung again and again, the edge chipping into the living wet wood more slowly than she expected. Her gasps for breath were swallowed by the slursh of the rain. The little tree finally tipped and sprawled, wood shards littering the dark new dirt Frederick had loosened around the tree base, downward branches making divots in the grass.

Priscilla threw the maul down. She slumped to her knees in the soaked grass. Frederick regarded her from inside the tunnel of his rain hood. She looked back at him, expecting anything—him to slap her, leave, call the police, summon a mental hospital. What had brought her here to her knees offered its bitter strength to Frederick, and Priscilla held her wet face up to him for whatever consequence he might deliver. She was calm and willing to bear openly the misery she had been keeping at bay.

Frederick moved the downed tree with the toe of his boot. "It wasn't going to make it," he said. "You probably did it a favor."

"You loved that tree," Priscilla said. "Didn't you love that tree?"

He shrugged. "I was trying to."

"You loved it, and I killed it."

Frederick came near and bent over her, dripping. "Yes."

"Then we're even."

Priscilla got to her feet. Frederick helped her. When their eyes met again Priscilla did not see the hurt or hatred she was expecting. Rather, his look had an animal attentiveness, hungry to come near but wondering how to survive the approach. He would forgive her the meat-eating, the tree slaughter, the secrets, but only if she would come back across the gulf between them into the unconditional lovelock they'd had around themselves. When they forsook all others to marry, back on the day Frederick bruised Priscilla's hands during their vows, they also forsook their pasts, their lives apart. With his pleading stare, Frederick asked this of Priscilla again, that he would forget the divisive events of the past months if she would. She wondered if she wanted that, if she was willing to relinquish the textures of what she'd gained and squandered. She let her stare back at Frederick reveal her new inner ruin.

She bent and picked up the maul again, amazed at its weight. She needed two hands on its end just to right it, handle-up. "Here," she said to Frederick, gesturing at their sheltered woodpile. "It's cold. Chop us some firewood."

And while he did so, Priscilla went inside and sat down by the fireplace, making a nest of newspapers and kindling for the stack of pine logs which Frederick brought in. She had a match lit and ready, and the old paper and dried-out sticks and logs caught fire within seconds. Together, with Priscilla's cold, muddy clothes congealing around her, she and Frederick watched the firelight grow and penetrate the indoor gloom, as though some script for how to live and what to say next might appear to them on the charred back wall of the fireplace.

8 Brittle Roses

It wasn't ever a mother thing. Let me get that straight. I mean, if you're a young woman and you love an older woman with big breasts, supposedly you have a fucked-up relationship with your mother. I've heard that, but in my case, it's bullshit. In fact, I have a pretty decent relationship with my mother, as long as I don't pull dyke attitude when I go visit her. Mom used to like hearing about where I went with Penna when she was on tour: the glittery cities on the West Coast, England, France, even to Prague and Rome & other hip cities in Europe. Mom knew I slept with women, with Penna, but if I ever mentioned it, she'd say, "Oh, Jane," as if I was afflicted with a big ugly birthmark or hairy nostrils or a crippled leg.

But I'm not crippled. Besides, I know about being crippled. I've been up close to disease and real pain like nobody's business. Penna has lupus. I could be a nurse. Even though Penna had a full-time groupie nurse for a while, for a long time I was the only one Penna would tolerate near her when she was having her worst flares, when her face puffed up and she couldn't even put her arm through a sleeve without help. She said the lupus made her feel rusty, and I'd joke about oiling her the way they fixed up the Tin Man in *The Wizard of Oz*. Sometimes she'd laugh, but most of the time she didn't. Sometime she'd manage a zoned-out smile. I took the drugs, too, once in a while. Darvocet for pain, and Xanax for the nerves. They make your body feel like some distant relative, or like waking up from a nap when you're a kid.

I was a cocktail waitress when I met Penna. In a small Indiana college town, where big gigs like the Indigo Girls and Lyle Lovett would blow in during midweek if they had time and felt like it between Chicago and Atlanta or Washington, DC. She was on the rise then, Penna Rae Graysender and Her Willful Wildcats, a sort of loud punk-country band with more ambition than good musical sense. Later they shortened their name to just Penna Gray, and started turning her long poems about not-quite romances between Vietnam vets and high school teachers into moody, funky ballads. That's when they started to make it big. Plus Penna got more interesting. Sometimes she'd dress like a guy and other times she'd put on low-cut Dolly Parton stuff. And then she'd come on to both women and men in the front-row audience. She could be everybody's or anybody's. And her voice, well—her voice was so crazy that you tasted it and felt it at the same time it bashed against your ears.

I was just twenty then, and she was forty-five, and I was finally admitting to myself that I wanted to be with women, and being gay was still thought of as an illness by way too many people. Still, I'd read that old dyke chestnut, *Rubyfruit Jungle*. I'd made out with a few girls, though I was discovering that women could be just as fucked up about relationships as they complain men are.

But one night I served Penna and her band Bud Lites as they rehearsed for their first gig in Bloomington and at the break between sets. She scarcely looked at me—in fact, I got more attention from her wiry drummer than from her at first—but after the show, about twelve-thirty, she came up to me while I was wiping down tables. "Are those great arms from doing that?" She sat down at the table and watched my sponge go round and round.

"Sorry?" I said. She was bigger up close, fragrant with sweat from her show. It had gone well—dance floor crowded, all those faces cheering, clapping, hips swaying, flipping their soggy hair back and forth.

She bared one of her own arms and made a Popeye-style bicep. "You lift?"

It took me a minute. "Sure. I lift beers, and scotches, and cheap wine, and—"

She laughed. "I don't suppose there's any place in this town where you can get coffee in the middle of the night."

"Nope." There was a Denny's by the state highway. "You could come over to my house," I said, not quite sure where I got the nerve to say it. "I've got some good stuff my brother sends me from California. He thinks I'm in a cultural wilderness."

She had the darkest blue eyes I'd ever seen. "Got enough for the whole band?"

"Yeah," I said. "I do." And after she went backstage to help the band finish wrapping up, I kept finding myself smiling as I finished my shift, appreciating the strength in my ropy arms, maybe for the first time.

When she and the band came over, my crummy little duplex turned into a happy place for a while. Even the woman renting the other side of the house, who often complained when I got home late and played the stereo however quietly, came over and drank coffee with us. Penna did imitations of country singers, including a version of "Achy-Breaky Heart" complete with curled lip and hip jerking, and her drummer asked my neighbor for a date. When they all got up to leave, the birds were cranking up outside in the gray light, and I didn't feel even slightly tired.

Penna took my hand at the door and kissed me on the cheek, just a whisper from the corner of my mouth. "What do you want to do with your life?" she said, under the goodbyes the rest of the band were hollering at my neighbor.

"Have adventures," I said. And then I thought about it. Was that true? There I was, art school dropout, waiting tables and growing old on cigarette smoke. Some adventurer I was.

Penna nodded, holding back a smile. "They can be arranged," she said. She unbuckled and slipped off her watch, a green and pink Swatch. "Oops," she said, handing it to me. "I must have misplaced my watch. Will you keep it safe until I get back?"

I put it on. The thick plastic band was still warm from her arm. "Of course," I said. "I'm sorry you'll be missing it."

"See you," she said, as her beefy bass player hustled her away. "Miz Graysender needs her beauty rest," he said. "Thanks for having us in." And then they were gone.

I slept the morning away wearing nothing but Penna's watch. That ticking explained to me at last why people put clocks into the beds of puppies away from their moms that first night. Anything that steady, even battery-driven, seems like perfect love.

*

Lupus is a motherfucker. Most of the people who get it are women. A big percentage of its victims are Black women, but it doesn't overlook aging white dykes—though you'd think both groups of people would've had enough to deal with in their lives.

If you've got it, you get rashes on your face, and you run mysterious fevers and bone-cracking flus for weeks. Your HIV test comes back negative. Every other regular test comes back negative. After about a hundred more tests, they finally figure out you've got it, and if you're lucky the drugs they give you make you go into remission. If you're not, you die young of heart problems or lung disease. You can't catch it from anybody, no one can cure it, and no one really knows what causes it.

With lupus, doctors tell you to rest. They tell you not to get excited. They give you barrels of drugs, some of which keep you up all night, so you also have to take sleeping pills. You're a walking medicine chest. You can lose hair, shake, and get face-bloat from the shit that's supposed to make you feel better. And you are totally not yourself.

*

I didn't hear from Penna right away after that first time I met her. Which actually was fine with me. I started thinking about the lines around her eyes, the sags in her chin. She was probably old enough to be my mother. I didn't have a thing for older guys when I was still convincing myself to go out with men. Older women? Same—nope.

But after meeting Penna, I dreamed about her body, all soft and yummy like the women in those 18th-century paintings. I craved her even while I was thinking, Jesus, she's too freeking old for you, she's two inches shorter than you, she's even built like your mother, etc., etc. At night, in bed by myself, though, I thought about touching her on top of her clothes. Then with clothes off. I imagined her hands on me. It's something for two women to touch each other's breasts. You know what she's feeling because she's making you feel it, too.

During the day, though, I had wars with myself about wanting to see her again. I stopped wearing the watch after about a week. It was just too weird. And when the days passed and I didn't hear from her, I was relieved—at least my mind was relieved. The rest of me had other ideas. My body ached. I woke up stiff. I took a lot of aspirin.

You know, though, the body has limits. By the three weeks later, I'd stopped thinking about her every half hour and just taken to wondering what might have happened with her. But then there were roses—ten of them, light orange—and a United Airlines airfare voucher to anywhere in the contiguous United States. And a note: "To a sweet bar girl with adventure on her mind. Use the travel however you want. I'm playing at the Warfield in San Francisco June 21. Penna." My neighbor had kept the roses in her side of the house until I got home around midnight, when she brought them to me, smiling. I guess Penna's drummer was calling her from the road pretty frequently, keeping her up later. "He must be quite a guy," she said of my rose-sending admirer.

"I've never gotten roses before," I said. "Orange ones, look. Aren't they weird? Orange roses." And before I had to explain anything, I quickly took them inside. I wasn't sure if my neighbor would believe who they were from, or even if I did.

Over the next bunch of days I fussed over them like they might grow. When they got droopy, I put them my back porch window sill to dry out. I tied them together with a satin ribbon, their petals papery like old skin. There's a photo of me and Penna somewhere holding the dried bouquet and each other, kissing. Along with the watch, roses were only the first of all the things she gave me.

*

They call lupus an autoimmune disease, but it's not like AIDS. Not at all, though that's what people think when you say "autoimmune." In fact, what happens is instead of crapping out, your body decides to kill you. Your body fights itself instead of some virus or bacteria.

But about six months into Penna's symptoms, even as worried as I was, I had to say that usually she looked great. In fact, though I'd heard lupus was one of the nastier diseases, I began to think maybe someone had miscalculated. Or that Penna, with her magnificent body, was going to fight it off. Right after they finally diagnosed her, we cried and yelled, but at least we had an enemy. Penna wasn't touring, and she took a month-long break from recording the next album. She'd had three pretty big hits on the most recent one, so we all figured she could take a breather without any career damage.

I squeezed her fresh grapefruit juice and massaged her every day. And when she began to feel better, we made love every day, too, the way we had when we were first together. You'd think after eight years you might not fuck the same body with so much relish, but Penna's illness gave me new concentration. I thought I could cure her by slapping my love all over her like lotion. Kind of a cheesy idea, I know. But you think this stuff when you're just nuts with love and compassion. And fear—for your sweetheart, and probably most of all, for yourself.

So I took a United flight to San Francisco for Penna's show. I had a moment of wondering if I should, but it didn't last long. I didn't know if I should let her know I was coming, or even how I could if I wanted to. I was a little young, remember. I just went, and bought a ticket like everyone else, and sat way off to one side in the Warfield Theater, jammed to the gills with twenty year olds. I guess she and her band were catching on, at least among the university crowds on the coasts. People were screaming and jumping around like it was the Stones coming on even before the roadies finished setting up.

And then Penna ran out, in these hip-deep yellow-and-black lizard boots, black jeans, and a black V-necked western blouse cut so low you could see her gorgeous boobs crashed together like a baby's butt. I had a physical shock down to my gut and lower, and then, with the kids screaming around me, I yelled and clapped and stomped just like everyone else. Penna whipped the mike cord behind her and belted out song after song. She sang some lyrics right at people in the audience, and others over their heads to the dark ceiling, to the night outside. I didn't know if she'd seen me or not, but part of me hoped she hadn't. I was afraid of seeing her up close, of finding her old again. But it was easy for me to love her when two thousand-plus people around me were loving her too.

During the break at the end of the first set, when everyone was milling in and out of the lobby, a man in an unreadable brown uniform touched my arm. "Would you mind coming with me?"

"Why?" He looked like the most he might be in charge of was a bread truck. "You a cop?"

He smiled like I was half-witted. "No, ma'am." People were squeezing around us. He lowered his voice. "Backstage." He flashed a photo badge. "You're requested backstage."

"Oh." I said. My guts suddenly felt a little watery. "Okay." I followed him, as meekly as if I had been arrested. I suppose, in a way, I had.

Penna was breathless and grinning when she saw me. "Clear a path!" she said to her crew, hovering over her like she was a race car. The sea of them parted and a chair materialized at her side. "Hi, sweetie," she said, cradling my chin and kissing me right on the mouth, in front of everyone. I suppose it could have been interpreted as a sisterly kiss, or just a very friendly one. But I didn't feel it that way. "God, I'm delighted you're here!" she said, still sounding out of breath. "Are you having fun? Aren't these college kids a kick in the ass?"

"Say, Penna, this your daughter?" A middle-aged guy swaggered front of Penna. I assumed he was her manager, or someone else all self-important. It was mutual hate at first sight. Plus it was just the first time the world tried to read us as mother and daughter. Which meant that we were not only dykes but potentially incestuous dykes. I gave the guy my fiercest glare, but I broke out in a prickly blush.

"Fuck you, Elmo," Penna said. "This here is my friend, Jane E. Katz, flown out at considerable trouble from Bloomington, Indiana."

Elmo squinted at me, as if putting me in focus might do me some good. Then he shook his head. "Whatever," he said, striding away.

"Don't mind him," Penna said. "He's a prick. But he's a good manager, mostly." She toweled her sweaty hair. "Look, tell Sydney to put you in one of the empty rooms set aside for me. Go get some sleep. I'll see you later."

"My stuff's at the Motel 6 on Van Ness." It seemed like the last chance I'd have to turn back.

She waved the half-protest away. "Tell Sydney to fix that, too." Penna flagged down a thin blonde woman with a big fluffy hairdo. "Yo, Sydney! This is Jane. Take care of her, would you?"

Sydney took my arm as if I were the new girl in class. "Well, now, what can we do for you?"

"I'll be singing for you, sweetie," Penna said, her attendants helping her into her second-set attire, much butchier than her first outfit: red jeans, red shirt, black jacket and boots. She was still buttoning as they hustled her down toward the stage.

Sydney's face was pert, ready for orders. But her skin had the leathery quality of too many years and too many cigarettes. Her orange lipstick was leaking into the wrinkles draining away from her lips. "I need a dose of sense," I said.

"Excuse me?"

"I mean, I need a bath and a drink. And my stuff from the Motel 6."

Sydney barely heard me finish before whirling away. "Coming right up," she said. "Follow me." And when I did, through all the backstage people and equipment and smoke and noise, and endless tiny rooms, it seemed that I really had left what was passing for my life behind. Coming was a jet take-off with a daredevil in the cockpit.

*

I never thought I'd live forever. I just thought I'd feel good for a long time, and that there would always be possibilities. I knew Penna would die before me. I used to look at old people, women in their eighties, and think, that'll be the cheek I'll kiss when she's eighty and I'm fifty-five. But it'll be Penna's cheek, the special cheek, starting its sag off her bones, but still hers.

What I hadn't factored in was disease. When her flares got more frequent than the good spells in between, Penna would cough, and speak crazily out of her night fevers, and shove me away when I tried the gentlest embrace. I got out those old orange roses she'd sent me that I'd dried and put them on her nightstand, but she was so feverish and confused that she couldn't remember where they were from. She'd shriek for quiet when I'd play even her favorite music, Patsy Cline and Mahler and early Elvis. The house in upstate New York we had gotten together, within walking distance of a swimming pond, was big enough for me to go elsewhere and play music, and break things and scream if I wanted to, which I did sometimes, just to hear a sound that wasn't Penna moaning or me talking to myself. I could see friends, but I really didn't want to be with anyone but Penna.

And Penna was full of something else, that was so possessive of her attention that I couldn't even get it from her or reach her through it anymore. She took chemo drugs they thought might help, which as you might have guessed made her throw up and drop weight like a political prisoner. On good mornings of her flares, when she had an hour or two of feeling well, she'd say, with her blue eyes scary-bright, "Teach me to draw." I'd try, but in the feverish hours following in the afternoon and night, she'd forget everything I'd taught her, and I'd have to start over again. And those were the good days. There were more days when she didn't ask for me at all, when her nurse, a smarmy know-it-all named Frances who had every single one of Penna's albums—tapes and CDs—fed her and bathed her. Sometimes I'd help. But sometimes not.

I was just under thirty. I'd think, in my most selfish moments, about possibilities, and about feeling good, the way I always had. I still had those, didn't I? I'd cry into drapes, kick furniture. Didn't I? God damn the world. And God damn Penna, for getting sick. For ruining our life together. For ruining my life. For being helpless. For being fucking mortal, after all.

*

The morning after I had let Sydney practically tuck me into bed in one of Penna's reserved rooms, I was so disoriented that I worked the knock on the door into a dream about trying to get out of the locked jewelry case I used to keep on my dresser as a kid.

"Jane?" It was Penna. "You hungry?"

"Yeah," I said, scrambling for my robe. "Hold on." I'd imagined myself naked with this woman more times than I could count, but there I was, covering myself up like a fifteen-year-old suburban virgin. It was a good thing I did, after all, because when I opened the door, there was a hotel guy with a room service cart. Penna stood behind him in ordinary jeans and a t-shirt.

"Well," she said. "You're hungry, here's food. Hope you don't mind if I join you." She shooed the hotel guy away and poured the coffee herself, her hand shaking just enough to tell me she was feeling the same crash of excitement and terror. "Here," she said. "I remember you like it black."

I took it. It was hot and good, but something felt strange in the room between us. Penna was watching me. My hunger for everything evaporated. Here I was, with this older woman I barely knew, who in the flesh was much more vivid and changeable than any of my fantasies, trying to dazzle me with her growing fame and wealth—for what? Did she just want a fuck-doll? And *was* I looking for a mommy figure?

"This is weird," I said. The coffee bit my tongue. "I don't mean the coffee."

"Yeah, I know," she said. "But there's no way to get to know somebody without going through weird. And I want to know you. It's not real complicated."

I was seeing that loose skin on her neck again. Not terribly loose, but not firm. Forty-five-year-old woman skin, you know. "There are always complications," I said. "I've dated some recently."

She leaned forward, put her coffee down. "Jane, let's eat breakfast. We don't have to be lovers, now or ever. Maybe you have a nice breakfast with me and fly home this afternoon. Fine. Truly—that's fine. We will both have had our adventure, and that will be that. But let's just get as far as toast, okay?" She took the silver cover off one of the plates.

"You think I'm some scared little girl, don't you?"

"I'm a scared little girl, too, you know."

So we ate our fancy eggs, and talked, and she asked me all about art school and why I had given it up, and about my mother, and about how my father lived in Portland, and how I used to ride horses, and about the old L.A. punk bands like X that I used listened to. Penna told me how she was married for a while, and her ex sometimes came to her shows, and about how her son was a teenager with musical ambitions of his own, and how she loved to swim.

By the time we finished everything on the tray, me even eating the parsley, our stories eased things up between us, making it natural for the two of us to go walking along the San Francisco Marina, pointing at the kite-flyers on the grass and the overpriced souvenirs for sale on the street-vendors tables, the Bay breeze whipping out our hair and the sun roasting our necks.

And when we got back to the hotel, we stripped off our clothes and slid against each other in bed for some hours, trying things we'd tried before, or that others had tried on us, and all of it felt to me like going over a waterfall. It's a blur now, but what's still with me is that first mirroring of our bodies, our nipples kissing, hip to luscious hip.

*

After months of almost constant illness, Penna suddenly got well. No fevers, no aches, no coughs, and only faint scars from the rashes stayed on her face. But instead of wanting to get back in the studio and get rid of that fawning nurse, Penna decided she was going to cure her lupus. She and Frances the Nurse went to several new doctors, reached the limit of their help, and then went on to Chinese herbalists, chiropractors, and homeopaths. The homeopath gave Penna a slew of little white-pill remedies to take, wouldn't let her have garlic or onions, & insisted she go vegan. She had chiropractic adjustments. And she got bags of herbal stuff for Frances to brew for her, shit that looked to me like lawn clippings, that Penna was supposed to make tea out of and toss on down her throat.

She did it all, like a good girl. She ate burdock root. She went to meditation groups with Frances, and the Chinese herbalist came over every week. She seemed happier than I'd seen her since she and I first got together, or probably I was flattering myself.

Maybe she *was* happier now. I must have been expecting a medal, for patience, for hanging in there like a good girl, special, wonderful me, who would make Penna better. It's the only way I can explain how hard I criticized all the health regimes she brought home. I even started smoking again. I suppose being good for so long made me crack bad.

"You idiot," Penna said when she got a whiff of the smoke on my breath. "I don't even want to get near you when you smell like that."

"Your loss, lady," I said. "I'd rather be burned tobacco than the heap of yard waste you're turning into."

She whipped over to me faster than I'd seen her move in months and backhanded me right across the face. "Shut the fuck up."

I grabbed her wrists, now so scrawny, and gave her a shake. "Bitch," I said. "You old bitch."

She jerked her wrists away from me with surprising strength. "Get away from me," she said, lurching into the room that used to be her practice room but more recently was her sickroom, where Frances the Nurse got Penna through her worst nights. Penna slammed the door behind her and locked it. I followed her and put my face to the door that hid her from me, breathing the faint draft that came through the crack. I could hear the beep-beep-beep of the phone, and Penna's shaky voice say, "Frances?"

At that I kicked the door with all my strength. Later when my foot swelled, I drove myself to the ER to fix the bones I broke. Penna and Frances were murmuring behind the locked door when I got back, hobbling as quietly as I could with the crutches the hospital gave me. Even I got the irony of Penna whispering like a girl behind doors and me the feeble one, stumping around like an old woman just minutes from the grave.

*

You start to forget the good times. Disease beats shit out of life. After that show in San Francisco, Penna asked me to come with her on tour, and I did. For a while I kept my duplex in Bloomington, in case things didn't work out, but as the months went by it wouldn't have felt like home anyway. So I moved out of the house, got rid of most of my stuff, saved what was worth saving in storage. Like those brittle roses. I stashed away that green-and-pink Swatch, wanting to keep it perfect like the night we met.

Penna and I went everywhere, as she got more famous and crowds got bigger. We hung out with a lot of rock stars you've heard of and some you probably haven't, and went to every major American city and a whole lot of the minor ones. She convinced me to quit smoking and got me drawing and painting again, ordering paper and expensive inks and oils for me without my asking. And yes, she paid for everything, but while she was rehearsing, I'd go off and make art. It got to be my work again, like it used to be, before I lost hope that someone like me would ever be good at anything. I know—that sounds self-pitying, and it is. But when you're queer in this world you can't help but visit some of the world's distaste for you on yourself. Even if you're a decent queer. A law-abiding, hard-working, faithful queer.

Mostly faithful, anyway. I loved Penna every single second even while I was sleeping with the whippet-thin roadie with the crew that assembled Penna's band. Her name was Laney, and she was about my age and even looked like me a little, bony and tall. We'd been sort of flirty friends until after Penna and I had our big fight, after which Penna spent a lot of time with Frances locked up in her room.

Laney helped me get around as my broken foot was healing, and it wasn't long before we wound up in bed. But she was smart enough to dislike being my dope for missing Penna, no matter how great the sex. After several weeks she stopped phoning. After trying for the tenth time to get Laney, it finally dawned on me that she was dumping me in self-preservation. I sat down in the unused rooms of the house where I had my studio and thought about running away, or killing myself. Or both, in that order.

I stripped the pictures from the walls and squeezed my expensive paints all over them, smearing them into muddy streaks that looked like real shit. I took off my clothes and painted myself, smudging the walls with my tits, with my ass, and wrists and elbows and face. I mixed glue and paint and broken glass with a big palette knife and spread it over the windows. I sneaked into Penna's empty room and got those dried-up roses, which I crushed and stuck onto the wall with the glue and glass. I didn't give a shit that my hands started to bleed.

When it was done I took a shower, packed a couple of decent out-fits, and put the suitcase in my car, the car Penna had bought for me. I'd pay her back for it sometime. In the hallway mirror I was ten years older than the bar girl I used to be, but I could still wait tables, proba-bly. Somewhere. New York City. Nashville. I looked around for paper to write a note.

The sound of Penna's thick cough told me she was just around the corner in the living room. And then she came into the hallway. She looked terrible. Her whole face was puffy, as if she'd gotten a bee sting in the middle of it. The patches across her nose and under her eyes were shiny and raised, like burn scars. I hadn't seen her up close in almost a month.

I'm leaving, was all I could think to say, but I didn't say it. Instead I stood there and stared at her. She stared back, and from the clench of her jaw I could tell she was aching all over, that it even hurt to stand.

"I hate myself," she said. "God, how I hate myself."

I'd hated myself, too. It's what her love fixed for a while. When I made all those lovey promises and gave my body, I'd gotten myself back, a nice, spiffy version loved in return. But I couldn't fix her. Period. Maybe that's why I most wanted to get away. Spare myself how useless I was.

Later I would see her even weaker. I would get it that progression in a progressive illness means not-good change and no going back. But right then she froze for me, this beautiful, dried-up person I loved so much it made my stomach cramp. Whether I stayed or left, I would lose her. After that, all I'd have to fit all the nothing inside me. The only way in the world I could get big enough for it was to keep loving her, to love us and the bulldozer that was coming for us.

"I can't leave," I said.

"You should," she said. But she didn't move when I went to her and put my arms around her, and felt how feverish she was, and how sweet and familiar. We stood there a while, weeping and swaying softly, and when she started wobbling, I held her up and took her back to her bed. But at the door to the master bedroom she stopped and said, "Let's go in there," where we hadn't been together for so long, and we did. I undressed her and then myself, we got into bed and lay down, snuggled, and slept.

So I stayed, and Penna fired Frances the Nurse. When Penna saw what I had done to my studio, she declared it genius and wouldn't let me clean it up. I'm not so sure about the genius part, but I look at it sometimes, and its total nuttiness makes me feel better. Funny—what I most like about it is that I still have those roses, even though now they're unrecognizable.

Lately Penna's been in and out of the hospital, fighting a lung illness they're calling acute lupus pneumonitis. She might go into remission again, but if she doesn't, she'll die. We've talked about that, as best we can talk about anything, with Penna's breath so short. She wants me to go back to art school, and I agreed just to get her to shut up about it. Her son's around a lot now, helping out, and he's great. Even my mother came for a visit. She was great, too. My brother sent Penna coffee when he heard how she liked it those years ago. Everything shrinks for a death, like we all have to huddle up before we can let the sick one go. After she's gone I'll do something, and keep living. I can't even imagine how, at this point, but maybe it'll be like painting. You get an idea, sketch it out a little, and hope something takes shape.

9 Vacation

The liquid smash of the tempered glass in Jackson's snorkel mask could have been another wave crashing on the beach beyond the patio. But then Jackson snapped and kicked the snorkel tube with its glassless mask into one of the patio chairs. When we looked down from our third-floor lanai, his wife, Nancy, was nowhere in sight. Reid had been listening, scratching his beard the way he does when he's nervous. He took his sketch pencil and made a mark on the lanai railing, after two others already there: three. "This'll be Jackson's snorkel set number four," he said.

We were on our last married trip together, Reid and I. We agreed: in the age of divorce, friendship has to do more work, so when we decided to end our marriage, we thought a final trip would seal off the one way we had been together and begin the new way—distantly friendly, sexless, concerned with other things. We had already been there for months. Except now Reid didn't have to sleep twelve hours a day, his black hair and eyes almost continually frowzy, and neglect his freelance design assignments, in order not to feel the resolute vacancy between us. I could stop working endless extra hours at the art supply store to avoid both him and the same chasmal sadness. We were actually more cheerful, more solicitous to each other once the divorce had been filed. There seemed to be hope, a future. All that remained was the final division of our things, the move apart, and telling our best friends, Jackson and Nancy, who suspected no trouble between us beyond perhaps generic marital boredom.

I had come to know Jackson and Nancy through Reid, who had roomed with Jackson during college. The four of us had become so close that it was natural to think of taking a vacation together. Our Midwest town had been extra cold that January; a trip to Hawaii in April sounded pretty good to all of us. But no matter how well you can know your married friends, you can still find a close look at their marriage, such as you get when traveling together, full of ugly unexpected edges. I mean, all couples have differences. Jackson and Nancy were occasionally as querulous as anyone. What we hadn't expected were the earnest, spiteful, full-throttle arguments they had, often resulting in the kind of destructive expression that had claimed Jackson's third snorkel mask.

Nancy wasn't someone you'd expect to have differences with anybody; she was courteous, articulate, and carefully groomed. Even her pale skin had a lovely sheen to it that looked like a dull polish. Jackson was funny and charming, but more unpredictable. He was the sort of man who spoke with his whole body, the way children do until they grow self-conscious. He was the first person I ever saw kiss the ground, which he did after the four of us finally arrived at the beachfront apartment building on Maui where we'd rented space for two weeks. Nancy and Jackson looked so alike—tall, blond, lean—you'd have thought they were siblings, though that was where the similarity ended. Nancy ended their quarrels by falling silent and taking up something to do with her hands, only the muscular pulse in her fine jaw betraying any emotion. Thus deprived of conversation, Jackson would also resort to physical expression, except his version was as violent as Nancy's was quiescent. There was the series of snorkel gear casualties; there were her expensive sunglasses hurled out to sea. One night there was a glass smash whose source we never did identify.

It had fallen silent down in the patio apartment I put my feet up on the lanai railing, watching Reid thicken and darken the line he had made with his pencil. "I wonder what color snorkel tube he'll get this time," I said.

He shrugged his big shoulders and didn't look at me. I remembered when that response had bothered me, back months earlier when our marriage still registered the sting of silence and indifference. Instead of feeling fruitless pain, I wondered again what really had happened to us, though it was a question I'd had so many times and not been able to answer that it took on the abstract interest of an insoluble equation, like the value of pi. We had agreed that relationships can just die, that such was the nature of their organicism, that we wouldn't suffer for some ossified notion of marriage we'd seen kill the spirits of too many people we knew.

It was all right for relationships to end. Most do. People come and go your whole life long. It was sad, to be sure—yes, sad. But our determination to stay friends would redeem the sadness of divorce, would invent a new way of knowing someone else that didn't insist on the binarism of spouse-or-stranger. It would be good. I felt a little happier then, thinking this, wiggling my toes on the railing, looking out at the relentless blue of the sea beyond. In my peripheral vision Reid seemed hunched and brooding, but soon I wouldn't have to feel miserable about that anymore.

"I'm glad we weren't ever like that," I said, standing, wrapping a towel around my waist, over my swimsuit. "Want to swim?"

This time Reid looked at me, in a way that made me as self-conscious as if he had been a stranger. It wasn't a lustful look, exactly—in any case, we'd sworn off sex, which hadn't been all that interesting to us recently anyhow. His attention was more speculative, assessing, making me aware of my tiny breasts, too-big hips. I wanted him to stop looking—privately, at least. If he was going to look at me that way, let him do it in public, where his glance would dilute with the detached glances of real strangers. "Let's go out to the beach and swim," I said.

"If you want to," Reid said. He stood and disappeared into the bathroom to change into his swim trunks. It seemed he was in there a long time. I sat and waited at the table in our tiny studio apartment. The surf below seemed loudest to me when it ebbed, at the sizzling end of each surge up the beach.

When Reid emerged from the bathroom I jumped up and nearly knocked over my chair. He was clean-shaved for the first time since I had known him. We'd been married five years, dated a year before that, and always, the beard was there. Ages ago I had tugged on it with my teeth when nuzzling him. Lately it had just etched the jawline and mouth of someone I saw more often from across the room. And now it was gone, and eyes I knew looked out at me from a grim, smooth, soft-chinned face that I didn't know. "Jesus, Reid!" I said. "What—what happened to your face?" I noticed he had a number of small acne scars I'd never seen before, little adolescent wounds, over the newly bared skin.

He stroked his cheek. "I want to tan there," he said. "I want to see what I look like tan there."

"It's cute, I mean, it's nice, it's—it's okay." I wanted to touch the new smoothness, but I kept my hands to myself. "What possessed you?"

"I just felt like it," he said. "I don't have to consult you about it."

"No, you don't," I said quickly. "That's true. No one said you had to." We were almost arguing, but about what? We were past argument, past resentment and hurt. Weren't we?

"All right then," he said. "Let's go."

I followed him down the stairs and kept my distance. Such was the awkward way of adjustment, I told myself. We were coming apart, after all, which was probably as unpredictable and difficult as coming together.

The savage midday sunshine tore at my shadowy thoughts. The sunlight in Hawaii has a menace to it I'd never experienced anywhere else—you can even get a sunburn underwater. But the plumeria trees at the base of the stairs shook out their white blossoms' sweet scent with the wind, softening the sun-brittle air. When we got to the water's edge I stripped off my towel, anxious to get in right away and feel the comfort of the water's salty buoyancy.

But Reid turned and called "Hey!" up the beach. Over his shoulder I saw a pair of identically untanned blonde people coming toward us, holding hands, smiling: Jackson and Nancy. "Look who's finally come out of their hole!" he said, too loud for only my ears. He broke away from me to go to them. They pointed at Reid's beardless face and laughed.

I remembered the first time I met Nancy and Jackson with Reid, and how complete the three of them seemed together. We had gone bowling. Reid and I were a team, but all three of them were so much better at it that I wished I had volunteered just to keep score. I smoked half a pack of cigarettes, something I hadn't done in years. "You really are a lousy bowler," Jackson had said to me cheerfully, and everyone laughed except me. I had flicked my cigarette ash and said, "Who gives a shit?"

"Jackson says we should go to Makena," Reid said when they reached me on the beach. Nancy and Jackson had an embarrassing glow about them, a wholesome, scrubbed look erasing the glass-strewn ugliness of an hour ago, the kind of freshness couples get just after sex. "Big, tough waves," Jackson said to me. "We gotta go check it out." Nancy beamed at him as though he'd said something clever.

"Okay," I said, though it almost didn't seem necessary that I consent, from the way the three of them were smiling together. I wondered if I would lose Jackson and Nancy, the coherent, familiar substance of the two of them, in divorcing Reid. But no, I was sure—this divorce wouldn't lose anything, except the pain of people who no longer wanted to be married.

We loaded up beer and various things to eat in the two big coolers from our apartments, packed beach chairs, towels, and straw hats, the usual stuff that always seems to make a beach trip even to a new place familiar and domestic. Reid drove, saying little, and I sat in front with him, while Nancy and Jackson rode in back, singing horrible old surfer songs and laughing. We passed several huge hotel complexes fronting the ocean, so sprawling and enormous they seemed connected to each other like a crappy strip mall.

After consulting the map, Reid turned south on a rough, only partially maintained road, flanked on either side by acres of forty-foot-tall prickly pear cactus and dry, stiff kiawe trees. At points through the cactus and trees there were piles of dark lava visible up on the lurid green slopes of Haleakala, the 10,000-foot tall dormant volcano that had created Maui millennia ago. Where these slides neared the road, you could see the spiky chunks of tar-black rock making up the dark piles. "We've gone off the end of the world," Jackson said. "'Soon gravity will leave us." It did seem like whatever rarified civilization that had spawned the string of hotels hadn't the courage for this rough place. I hoped our flimsy rental car, lurching over chuck-holes, had enough air in its tires, oil in its crankcase.

Finally there was a little hand-lettered sign, *Big Beach*, with an arrow pointing right, along with several official-looking signs: *Warning Strong Current Dangerous Shorebreak*. We pulled into a packed-dirt parking lot, already occupied by a dusty VW van and a couple of other nondescript passenger cars with surfboard racks clamped to their roofs. A big group of Hawaiians was crowded around the van, some barbecuing on a little hibachi and others, kids mostly, running back and forth from the ocean. The adults nodded to us as we unloaded our gear, though a few men scowled when Jackson swung away from us to go by the van and call out, "What's for lunch?"

He caught up with us as we waded through the deep sand. "God, leave people alone, Jackson," Nancy said, low. Her extra-dark sunglasses masked her eyes.

"Leave who alone?" he responded. We were now well out of earshot of the Hawaiians and several yards along the beach. "You mean those people way back there by the van I just said hello to? You're a little late, aren't you? Come on, let's go back there and I'll get out of the car again, and this time you can get me before. I sin by speaking to a bunch of people standing around a van having a barbecue, okay?" He threw the lawn chairs he was carrying into the sand. "Come on, let's go back. Let's go make it right."

Nancy's lips barely moved. "Don't be a asshole, Jackson."

"Hey, I'm trying to be an accommodating guy! Whatever you want to do—I'll do it. Your wish is my command. Let us undo what has been misdone." Jackson fell to his knees in the sand and bowed to her—bowed to all of us, actually, since Reid and I were right next to Nancy. Neither Jackson nor Nancy had explained or even mentioned what was bugging them, what was driving them to their fights, but I had the feeling we were suddenly in the presence of whatever it was, however unspoken it might remain. It was something they believed they were through with that clearly wasn't through with them, something that in its unarticulated state could inhabit any imprecise conversation, any mind's shadow.

Her jaw clenched, Nancy said nothing. She turned away and walked further across the beach. I turned to follow her, hearing Reid say, "Hey, man, come on."

Whatever verbal response Jackson may have had was lost to me under the shuddering whump of a tall, straight dark wave curling on the steep beach. Nancy and I stopped to stare; it must have been at least fifteen feet high. The same waves came here as did to other parts of the island, but the slope of this particular beach, so the tourist brochure told us, was such that even average waves could build up to unusual heights and fall in a straight curtain, which only the nuttiest surfers attempted. It was one thing to read this in the brochure, and another to actually witness the force of the water: the undertow after each wave so strong it was like a fast river flowing down the sand.

The three of us continued along the beach, turning our backs on Jackson. I was a little behind and to the right of Nancy, and Reid was behind me, when I heard Reid say, *Jesus shit.* Before I could have another thought, all my senses shut off for a second as if I'd blown a fuse. The next thing I knew I was sitting in the sand with my head and shoulders tangled inside the aluminum and nylon-mesh of a beach chair, which Jackson had flung and intended for Nancy. Reid was next to me, saying, *God dammit, Jackson,* in a hard voice over and over. Nancy was standing in front of me, crying, and Jackson as carefully pulling the chair away from my face and out of my hair, saying *oh, baby, I'm so sorry, God, I'm so sorry, you're all right, aren't you? Please forgive me,* crooning in my ear like a lover.

I was dizzy, and Jackson was very close, and I didn't know him very well, really, but no one had ever touched me the way he did right then, first having hurt me and now mending me, opening up the hurt of the moment to get at all the hurts I'd ever had, trying to touch and soothe them, too. His fingers were nimble and soft. His fair, blue-eyed face was right near mine, and I became Nancy for a confused moment—

looking into a mirror of my own face, at someone who loved me and hated me as thoroughly as he loved and hated himself. Like a brother, or a child, he was someone I couldn't deny; like a body in the throes of illness, his need for my attention was urgent and uncomplicated. I didn't love Jackson—I knew him only as an element of Jackson and Nancy. But I knew then why it might be hard not to love him, hard for Nancy to keep herself distinct from the force of his need for her. It would be like trying to elude the crush of gravity, or the pressure of water at great depth.

My dizziness passed, and another big wave vibrated the sand beneath us. Reid was beside me, and our beach things were scattered all around. "You're not cut anywhere," Jackson said, very quietly. "Do you feel all right?" I put my hand up to a place high on my forehead that throbbed. "It's a little red there—you might have a bruise," he said.

"I'm fine." I tried to focus, looking directly into his eyes. "You really are insane," I said, though my voice was unsteady, and it didn't sound very insulting.

He looked left and right, then whispered, "The truth is, I'm really an alien." He stroked my head. "Krista, I'm so, so sorry. Please forgive me. I know not what I do, most of the time."

"It's okay, Jackson," I said. I moved to get up, and the two men helped me. Nancy squeezed my hand, wiping her eyes under her glasses, her mouth twisting into a tight smile for a moment. Then she turned to Jackson. "I hate you," she said. She took about ten steps away, opened and set down her beach chair, and knelt beside it in the sand, sitting inside her turned-up feet the way flexible children can. As Jackson went over to her, she began grabbing and emptying handfuls of sand. I didn't hear what they were saying, but I could see the angry purse of her mouth as she faced out to sea.

Reid opened and arranged, another chair, the same one that had hit me, in fact, and guided me to sit in it as if I were very old. "God, what an asshole," he whispered, getting his own chair set up next to mine. "You okay, honey—I mean, Krista? Do you want to go back to the apartment? Can I do anything for you? Do you want a beer? Man, I'm so sorry."

He looked like such a boy squatting there in front of me, long arms and legs all folded on themselves, just like the boy Jackson was, throwing a beach chair at his wife in a tantrum and missing, maybe not really meaning to hit her at all but hitting someone nonetheless. And then there was Nancy, sitting there in the sand like a child, waiting for Jackson to seduce her out of her sulk and promise to love her up again later in their apartment behind silent drapes. What a strange way to be married! That wasn't the way Reid and I had been as a couple at all. We had been proud of our marriage's ease. We smiled when friends praised our compatibility. We had been calm and mature. Wasn't that the way married people were supposed to be?

Reid was still squatting in front of me; his legs had to be feeling the strain. "Just go away," I said. "Please."

He sighed. "Okay," he said, getting to his feet. Jackson had moved away from Nancy and gone toward the water, and Reid met him at the wet sand's edge. They talked for a while, gesturing back and forth, the surf swallowing their voices. Then they stripped off their shirts and tossed them up the beach. "We're going to try some bodysurfing," Reid said.

"Which is another way of saying, 'we'd like to be ground to a pulp, please'," Jackson added. They laughed. I watched another tall wave set up its dark ridge, draw water away from the shoreline, hang crested for a suspended second, and then smash itself onto the beach. "You guys are out of your minds," Nancy said, not smiling, though her voice was lighter than before. I said nothing, though I agreed with her. But I wasn't going to play the game with them—the indomitable boys, not about to heed warnings, especially from women, stand-in mothers no matter what their age or childbearing status. Besides, Reid would soon be no one's husband, no one's worry. "You girls watch the beer," Jackson said. "If anyone comes, drink it all." Together they dashed for the water.

They reached the surf during what became a long stretch of short, mild-mannered waves that most fit adults could have managed. But then the crests came more slowly and built up, until one came that was so large that Kaho'olawe, the desert island eight miles away, vanished behind its profile. Standing in receding knee-deep water, Jackson pointed, and just a puff of his yell to Reid reached us. Both of them turned and faced the wave as it humped itself up, almost in slow-motion, though they took none of the usual precautions against a wave's full force, like preparing to dive under it or turning sideways. They just stood there, their hands reaching out, their faces almost touching the wave's glassy wall, before it collapsed around them into shapeless foam and they disappeared.

"Damn!" Nancy said, who had pulled her chair over next to mine.

"Yeah," I said. "What in the hell were they doing?"

Seconds passed; the spent wave shot way up the beach, nearly to where we were sitting with all the beach gear. Just as we were about to jump up to move the perishables, the surge slowed, lingered there as if to mock us, then rushed back into the wave line, leaving the beach behind it gleaming. And as a choke of terror that I hadn't expected rose in my throat and a shout full of Reid's name burst into my mouth, the two men rose out of the surf almost simultaneously. Laughing and spitting, they flipped back their wet hair the way it seems all boys do, with the jaunty, defiant jerk of the head that seems to say, you missed getting me again this time, mother water. The afternoon light was hard and Reid looked hard, his skin taut from the water's light chill. I felt a chill, too, though not from the temperature. He was this strange, beardless, muscular creature come from the sea, but at the same time he was mine, he was still my husband, he was part of me, and I felt myself inside him as he stood there dripping and coughing. "We saw ourselves," he said, breathless. "Amazing. We saw ourselves out there."

"What are you talking about?" Nancy said.

"Jackson," he said, breathing hard. "Jackson showed me this thing, this way to see a wave."

Jackson sat down panting on the sand. "If you stand in front of a big wave like that until the last minute, because it's so slow, if the light's right, you can see your reflection in it. And man, the light was really right." He took noisy breaths. "So cool, this paleish blob—your own face, right on the water wall." He slapped Reid's arm with the back of his hand. "Saw you, too, man. Saw both of us."

I saw it too, even though I hadn't really seen it. Sometimes what people tell you becomes your own, maybe because they tell it well, or because what they tell is something you need yourself. "So what kept the wave from creaming you?" I asked Jackson, though I didn't take my eyes off Reid.

"Oh, you curl up into a tuck and it bats you around a little," Jackson answered. "But you come up okay all the same." He stretched himself out on the bare sand, a handful of which Nancy flipped onto his wet belly. "Hey!" he yelled, flipping sand back at her. "I can do that too, you know. There's a lot of sand out here."

Reid sat down at my feet and, like a cat, started rubbing his smooth, naked face on my legs. "Get away from me," I said. "You're wet." Instead of heeding me, he stood and picked me up right off the chair. I kicked at him. "Asshole," I said, something I'd never called him or anyone. "Leave me alone."

"No," he said, laying me on the sand and pinning me down. "Sorry, baby. Here I am. Deal with it." It was odd talk for him, more like Jackson or some silly cool teenager trying to impress me. The sun blared in my eyes as the ocean still on him dripped on me, and I could barely see him except for the gleam of his teeth and the silhouette of his head. I dug my nails into his wrists; he responded by squeezing my arms until they hurt. I laughed, a little hysterically. I could hit him, really hard. I could bite and draw blood. Anything seemed possible right then. Lying there wincing under Reid, my arms bruising inside his fingers, everything puzzling about Jackson and Nancy seemed so simple to me, so elementary: sometimes you want to hurt the people you love because you can. It's one sure way of knowing that you matter.

Tears from the ache of my pinched arms burned in my eyes. Reid's dense body pressed me into the sand; he wasn't holding off any of his tall weight. "We're getting divorced," I said, the way I might have to Jackson and Nancy, breaking the news quietly and evenly at last. Though sprawled on the sand under a man I knew but whose face I could not read, the announcement seemed meaningless, irrelevant.

I lay there, helpless but fierce. *Okay,* I thought to Reid. *Hurt me——go ahead. Do it.* What difference could it make now, with a throttled marriage gasping in our hands? For the first time, I knew this divorce would hurt, more unfathomably than I had dreamed, the way accident victims bleed at last when rescued from crushing weight. But maybe you learn to love your scars—they tell you where you've been.

"Kiss me," I said, and he did, hard, his cheeks and chin as slick as those familiar lips. I didn't know what would happen next, but I had a glimmer of what sort of creatures each of us could become. We stared at each other; the moment held its breath. Slowly, we let go our painful holds.

10   We Keep No Animals

We grow our own food in soil innocent of artificial fertilizers, fungicides, or pest control chemicals.

Beth was reading over Lee's shoulder as he typed in with his two index fingers. He didn't much like her watching. But sometimes she couldn't help herself.

What hungry creatures we find on our plants we pluck off with our fingers and crush under our feet. Beth always felt regretful about this insect killing: the metallic Japanese beetles, copulating on a grape leaf; the green, ravenous tomato hornworms, slow and fat in their infant helplessness. Soft and rolling in the fingers like yarn.

The *we* was the two of them, Lee and Beth, working together on their remote Vermont farm, in 1931. They were living the way Lee thought everyone ought to live, his writings about it having made for him a modest fame. They dressed in the early morning, putting on clothes from the previous day. They would use fresh clothes only when the worn ones became stiff and sour. *We change only to prevent irritation to the skin, not for the vanity of having soap-scented clothes on our bodies every day.*

They would wake at the same time, or nearly. Beth imagined Lee's eyes open in the dark as soon as she opened hers. His were deep eyes of the clearest blue, like glacier ice she had seen in picture books. Lee had twenty years of seeing through them before she was born, a whole youth and shove to manhood without her even being alive. She imagined a moment that never happened, in which a twenty-year-old Lee stands in soft work clothes and receives a baby in his arms, and a voice from nowhere says, this is the woman you will love and live with one day. And the young Lee laughs in a tight way, as though he hadn't had much practice laughing, and hands the baby quickly back. *I don't think it will be so,* he says. *This gal is a little young.*

We eat simple grains and yogurt at breakfast. Though we don't exploit animals to get their milk, we have a neighbor down the road who takes good care of his cows. For their milk we trade him fruit. Beth would make yogurt and use the last half cup as starter for the new batch when Lee got her a bucket of fresh milk. Both of them had to walk carefully on the kitchen floorboards when the yogurt was curdling, as though trying not to disturb a sleeping baby. Curdling yogurt needs stillness and quiet and warmth, and if it's pestered it punishes you with runny, sour milk instead of yogurt. Beth wept at the first failed batch, halfheartedly jellied as coddled egg white.

This happened only weeks after they moved into their first house on the homestead together, a month after Beth's twenty-first birthday, on which she told her mother and father that they had quietly married at the courthouse in town. A lie. They had not married, for Lee did not believe in marriage anymore, though he was tender-hearted enough to afford a lie to Beth's mother and father, good people, farmers themselves back in their native Hungary. They were happy their girl was married away, difficult as it was to marry off girls sometimes. Beth's mother was one of six girls and lucky enough to be pretty and have strong arms.

We work four hours each day at house and garden, four on our own projects. Our books describe the subtleties of gardening, proper mulching procedures, cooking and eating in a self-sufficient household. Both their names went on these books: Lee and Beth Harrihold. Lee wrote the books mostly, sitting at a typewriter, picking out the letters he needed with his two index fingers. He became a fast typist over the years, faster than Beth ever was in the office job she had after high school. She washed jars or cooked or mended while he typed. *Everyone works in our household, even guests. No one shirks or gripes. We offer each other a hand when it's needed.*

When it was time for her to write he came to get her. If she came before he was ready, he typed on as if she weren't there. If she stood right near him, clearing her throat, finally saying, "I can write now," meaning, I want to write now, I want to say something, the jars are washed and put away, the soup can't be watched anymore, he looked up, puzzled, and said, "How is your book going?" He meant the one he sewed and bound himself for her for their first Christmas together: a beautiful thing, heavy with creamy, wide pages, a heart drawn in the corner of the front endpaper, next to the words, "Your Book, from your Lee." He had forbade her to enter the workshed in December that year, so she figured he was making her some tool, a shelf, a wooden wheelbarrow. But he had bought a secondhand book about bookmaking and got the materials during solitary trips into town. When she unwrapped the book, he had said, "For your watercolors and your own writing and such." She was amazed and pleased; she leaned to kiss him, and he kissed her back in the sort of quick, almost fearful way of his. She could tell from the tuck of his smile that he was pleased, too.

He sent her to her book this way when he was busy writing, and sometimes she went and sometimes she didn't, sometimes finding other things to do. But when he wanted her to come he'd look over his half glasses, smiling, eager as a child. "Here's a part for you to write, Betts," he would say. He knew what things she loved and saved those parts of the writing for her: animals, blueberry harvesting, soup-making, how to keep knives sharp.

We keep no animals. Big animals waste space, consume unnatural amounts of resources, and trample precious topsoil. Their dung attracts pests. Docile, overfed cats and dogs frighten away the more wild animals with whom we share the world. We will enslave no creatures.

They would have no animals in spite of the fact that most farmers have animals, farmers like Beth's own father. Beth remembered Poppa's stories about his boyhood—how cows in Hungary watched him sometimes and licked him when he was trying to milk them, and about the depth of their dark, marble-like eyes. The warmth and softness of newly hatched chicks. Pigs as big as a bed. Geese that guarded the house better than any dog. She thought about having animals like this one morning as she and Lee were turning the compost pile, though she knew how the discussion would turn out. But somehow she had to speak anyway. It was a way of hearing her own voice.

"Lee?" she said, intent on her pitchfork. It was nearly a year after they had taken possession of the farm. "How would it be to have a cow in the pasture near the creek?" The blueberries were growing well, the Jonathan apples hanging in boisterous clusters. They had just finished making a pond the week before.

Lee looked up at the bright sky and frowned, as if he disliked what was gathering there. "Just one cow," Beth added. "We can breed her to one of Orren's bulls, then give the calf away on the condition that the receiver not slaughter it. Then we'll have milk. Wouldn't it be nice, having our own milk?"

He glanced at her briefly, his face still full of its frown, then turned back to the compost. "I'm working on a section in the *Living Rightly* book this week," he said. "Think I'll need your help on it." She knew which book it was; she had already written the parts on preserving food and making salads with raw vegetables. She had been anxious to write something more. It had been a while—all this book was getting written without her having written hardly anything, it seemed. And her name would be on it with his. But she wasn't talking about writing.

"What does the book have to do with getting a cow?"

"Betts, animals make you dependent. They tear up the land. You know that. You wouldn't countenance buying a man for a slave, would you? Animals get enslaved just like men."

Beth had a childish urge to stamp her feet in frustration. She didn't want a slave, she just wanted a cow. "I wouldn't want to whip her or tug her around by the nose by a ring," Beth said. "For heaven's sake! Why get so riled up?"

Lee scowled. "I am simply saying to you, Betts, honey, that I love animals as much as you do, and I don't think keeping them helps them any." He shoved his fork into the dirt. "It's wrong," he said to the warm compost.

Beth was suddenly aware of his hands, firm around the pitchfork handle. They seemed rough and cruel, as unyielding as the wood they held. "Seeing's how you love animals so," he continued, "how about you write the part in the book about why we don't eat or keep animals?" He smiled at her. "I know you could write with real feeling."

It was something to write. She could see the words on the page, words she typed herself. When she was writing, Lee would keep well away from her, as though she were doing something special and private, like praying. And it felt that way, a little: wholly distracting, something that made her completely herself. She would return from this writing time as if from a refreshing trip, lighthearted and full. Lee always praised the results, saying she had a writing gift.

"All right," she said. She drove her fork into the ground and went to him, wanting to feel him, anyway, his skin and hair and lips. She put her arms around his neck and nuzzled his cheek, salty from the morning's sweat. He smiled and kissed her abruptly, using one arm to squeeze her, but as always he dropped the hug before she did, turning back to the work before she had loosened her arms from around him. She had grown used to that, she supposed.

They worked on in silence, as they often did. All the rest of that day, though, Beth couldn't stop thinking about a cow, or maybe a calf, or a goat, something with soft fur, maybe something even smaller, like a rabbit, or a cat. Or ducklings, two of which she could hold in her hands, their tiny hearts fluttering, their fluffy bellies warm and trembling.

When she and Lee began talking of homesteading, six months after they met, Beth assumed they would have animals like this, the way Poppa had. They were on a date, it was June of 1930, and Beth was twenty years old. Her parents were just a little amused at the attentions of this forty-year-old man for their daughter. They treated him like a boy, sitting him down in their wide hallway that served as a parlor, as he held a sprig of black-eyed Susans that he'd picked out of the vacant lot next to his room twelve blocks away.

Lee took Beth for ice cream. That was what young couples did. Beth let him fuss with her sweater, watched him jump to get it when it slipped from her chair, the plastic pearls twisted into its yarn making a ticking sound on the floor tile. He ordered a chocolate ice cream soda, making Beth almost invisibly duck her head, trying to resist embarrassment and failing—chocolate soda was all you needed to say, all anyone ever said. He sounded like a foreigner ordering, even though she was more foreign than he, the lilt of her parents' Hungarian accent always in her ears. The girls and boys in the ice cream store looked so young. She imagined them looking at her. Some of them she vaguely recognized from high school. She imagined the girls comparing their boys' hair with Lee's, noticing the gray at Lee's temples, the strands of gray in his eyebrows, the depth of the wrinkles under his eyes. They were the only couple so strange in the entire world.

But there was a powerful sense of God in Lee, something Beth had been looking for in everything and everyone else. Lee seemed to collect God in the way he sat, mindless of his appearance, his eyes fixed on her. She soon forgot any of his strangeness. He held in favor of the common man's rights, against empire, profit, waste, and war. He had protested aggressive government actions at rallies and had been dismissed from a job for his views. He wrote articles for radical journals, though he refused more than just enough money to live on. Even Beth's Poppa, suspicious of anyone critical of his adopted country, was impressed by Lee's concern for farmers and commitment to thriftiness. Moving air seemed to stop around Lee. When she beheld Lee, even from the first day she met him, Beth felt this way, as though she had swallowed something big. As if she stood at a doorway to another country.

When Lee reached out for Beth's hand that night on the ice cream date and covered it with his, Beth had sighed. A couple a bit older than Lee had come into the sweets store. He took her sigh as a sign of pleasure: this girl likes me some. In truth, Beth had only been relieved that he was no longer the oldest person in the store. So when he felt brave enough to say, "I've been thinking about us, together, Beth. You with me, and maybe the two of us farming somewhere together," she was still full of this relief. Its warmth melted into delight. She thought of her father and his stories about the animals. A farm life with Lee could be like living in her father's stories, with the big pigs and soft cows and mean geese. Together, she and Lee would live with their animals into their own stories.

They had already told each other hundreds of stories about themselves from Lee's forty years in the world, from Beth's childhood. Beth dreamed of finding God. She looked for God in animals' eyes and in the people she saw in the city. While other teenaged girls worried about silk stockings and how much wave they had in their hair, Beth went to churches at odd hours—four o'clock in the afternoons on weekdays, late Saturday night—and sat in the pews alone, listening. She wasn't sure what she was listening for, but she had a feeling that, if anything, God would come to you through sound: the way sound could be around you and behind you and above you, all at the same time.

Lee would listen to her while she talked like this, thinking, *I have found God, in the smooth face of this rare girl.* He would never have said such a thing to her—it would be frivolous. But he had tried marriage, and not found it easy. He had married Susana fifteen years earlier because they were like a team of perfectly matched horses, capable of pulling the weight of their dreams for improving the world. But then there was housework to do, and Susana knew how to do the cooking and the cleaning. And did it. It was miraculous to Lee that he would go away for the day to write or lecture, come back and find the house immaculate, dinner ready, and Susana writing in the few moments left before supper, her face flushed. He knew she had done it all herself. He was grateful for her efforts, the way a supplicant receives grace: he knows he's a sinner anyway, and that knowledge tinges his gratitude with shame.

Susana's views on the Woman Question became more and more polemical, finally arriving at the opinion that a woman could not be a housewife and be fully herself. She and Lee passed each other in the halls of their house without speaking. One day she said, "I'm thinking of moving to Philadelphia," and they were in Boston, and Lee could only think to say, "that's far from here." He had already begun to eat alone, teaching himself the rudiments of food preparation as if getting ready for some long, solitary trip, and to go out alone without announcing his destinations. And after Susana had left, he went into all the rooms of the house and said her name, as if calling forth her lingering spirits from furniture and wallpaper. He never bothered with a divorce from Susana, and she never asked for it. It seemed like a dream past belonging to someone else.

Especially after he had met Beth at the Theosophical Society of Boston meeting the January after Susana left for Philadelphia. Soon thereafter he saw Beth every week. Lee got to hold Beth, and after a while, to kiss her. Though he had been married all those years, touching Beth was frightening, like piloting a sled down a steep hill of the slickest snow, without being able to see the bottom or what lay there. Beth was not like him, as Susana had been—Beth was a thing of a foreign forest granting him rare audience. She was small and slim, but in the muggy summer nights her sleeveless blouses showed lean and muscular arms, shoulders broad for a woman. Lee had heard of a cheap farmhouse plus acreage up in Vermont; he woke at night dreaming of moving there and living on what his own hands could work from the land.

But the thought of going alone made him sweat with panic. And here was this girl who talked of God and listened when he spoke of organicism and socialism, and lay her small head on his shoulder as he guided her home from wherever they contrived to go just to be together. He had forgotten where they had been in those first six months. He only remembered her.

So they staged their false marriage, going out one Sunday afternoon in their best clothes without disclosing their destination. When they came back with their invented news and announced their plans, Beth's mother cried and kissed them, and gave them what small extra household items she had. She also gave them some ugly heavy clothing she had brought over on the ship when she and Beth's poppa came to America, clothes that delighted Lee for their very discardedness. He and Beth went north through New England by train for as long as they could, and when there were no more rails they hired a wagon to take them and their few things to their land in Vermont.

They spent their first night as real, physical man and woman in a barn loft, sweet with late summer warmth and ripened hay, a small corner of which was prepared as a makeshift bed by the family selling them the farm. Beth was startled by the veins standing out on Lee's legs, the looseness of the skin on his chest, but his arms were strong and sure around her. For his part, Lee was afraid of hurting her, she was so small, then he was afraid of impregnating her, and then he was just afraid. She never knew, but when he was spent, covering her body with his in the dark, he wept a few tears, sealing his life with Susana behind him forever.

That was the last time they had intercourse without taking great care to avoid pregnancy. They had not talked of children, though Beth knew of Lee's son and of Lee's strong beliefs about world overpopulation. It was just that Beth always thought she would be a mother. She had grown up mothering her parents, the succession of cats all named Mitzi that her mother took sporadic care of, other children in the neighborhood, her few friends through school as they endured their heartbreaks over boys lost and poor grades earned. And as the Vermont farmhouse took shape around them, with Lee hammering and sawing and relaying stone foundation, Beth only had Lee to mother. She mended his old clothes and helped him with as much of the construction work as she could, rubbing his neck and shoulders unasked at the end of the heaviest lifting days.

Perhaps he would want children later. It was a good thing to wait. Beth resolved to be patient.

A day or two after she had talked to Lee about owning a cow, Beth was making her way out to the compost pile with some kitchen trash. It was a leafy late afternoon, fall starting its creep across the valley, brushing the ends of tree branches with bright orange and red. The breeze was sharp and fresh in Beth's mouth. She was listening by long habit for the sense of God around her, though now that she wasn't a silly teenager anymore she knew that twig snaps and distant birdsong were signs of God; she wasn't likely to get trumpet fanfare or choirs of heavenly voices. She smiled at that old thought, at the girl she used to be, waiting for peals of holy laughter, or song, or whispers.

She did hear something in the bushes, next to the compost pile. They were far enough away from town noises that red fox, black bear, deer, rabbit, grouse, and wild turkey crossed their land from time to time. All they usually had to do was stand very still whenever they heard noises, and, often as not, whatever it was came out of the woods to look at them. *Our policy is not to pursue any wild creature, even just to look at it. Chasing animals is harassment, as bad as killing or eating them. We have respect for all life, even the most humble.*

But after Beth dumped the house scraps into the compost pile, she set down the pail and started into the woods after the noise. Lee was back in the house, cleaning the last of the wooden dinner dishes. She could imagine the soft skin of his chin and neck folding together as he bent over the sink, washing as if there were nothing more serious in the world than washing. She stopped for a moment and looked back toward the house. The light from the kitchen reached her in thin beams through the trees.

She kept going into the woods. The sound that drew her was a rustling, underneath an intermittent yip. To Beth's ear it was the sound of confinement, of fright, of being small and angry and desperate.

She only went about thirty feet into the thicket bordering the compost pile before she saw it, a raccoon, thrashing against an old rusted beaver trap closed around one of its rear legs. It was chewing around the trap with concentration, and it looked up at her almost in annoyance when she entered the thicket, as though she had disturbed something serious and private. The hair was all gone from the leg where the trap closed on it, and the tiny sharp teeth had begun to go into red flesh. When the blood ran, the raccoon licked it away. Beth saw that the trap wasn't attached to the ground the way the old traps were; the raccoon had been dragging the trap for yards or even miles. What path she could discern was in direct line with the compost pile, in which she had just dumped spoiled milk and a few burned ceci beans and tomato skins.

"Oh, little thing," Beth said, resisting the urge to go to it and try to pet it or pry open the trap. Among the many things Poppa had taught her about animals was that they fight when cornered or trapped, the more so the bigger the creature confronting them. Although she and her family had always lived in the city, Poppa kept rabbits and explained their behavior to Beth as she watched them. He would usually slaughter them when she was at school or on one of her church visits, though there were some weekends when they needed meat. Poppa was quick and efficient with the heavy wood club, killing the rabbit in a blow to head, slitting the furred skin around the neck, and pulling the skin off inside out like a tight suit of clothes. Beth tried hard to think about God's purposes for animals, the way animals eat other animals all over the world, and would they eat each other if God didn't want it, didn't in fact want his creatures to gain nourishment from each other?

Nonetheless she often cried on slaughter days, hiding her tears from Poppa, who would laugh and shake the guts at her if he saw her so weak and weeping. She named all the rabbits privately, petting them each the night before as a kind of blessing.

Though it was silly to cry over rabbits, she knew, and Poppa was just providing for the family the way good fathers do.

But Beth had the same desire to save the raccoon, to protect it from injury, that she had when Poppa was picking out rabbits on slaughtering day. Yet she couldn't touch the coon—not yet. You have to build the animal's trust first.

She quickly went back through the forest to the compost pile, behind which stood a little toolshed. From inside she pulled out a segment of chicken wire, from which Lee had made the enclosure for the compost pile. Then she leaned over the pile and picked up the ceci beans and some moldy bread, and half-ran back through the woods, wire in one hand, food in the other. The raccoon had advanced about another foot, this time starting back from her.

"Don't worry, I'm a friend," she cooed to the raccoon, who tried to drag itself away from her. "No, no, don't worry, don't be afraid." She rolled the chicken wire into as large a ball as she could and set it around the raccoon, making for it a small cage. The raccoon had to stay out in the woods. Lee must not know it was here or that she was taking care of it. He would—he would probably want to kill it, to put it out of its misery. He would look at Beth from under his eyebrows, scolding her without saying a word.

But Beth was going to see to it that the raccoon wasn't miserable. She poked the food through the wire, though the raccoon ignored it and set back to chewing at the trap. How she wished she could spring the trap! But it wasn't yet time—she was likely to get bitten, and that she couldn't hide from Lee. She had never hidden anything from Lee. She would see if the raccoon had eaten anything when she checked back the next day. Though she would have to be careful, for Lee might suspect if she were gone too long or too eager to run to the compost pile.

Lee suspected nothing that night, though he did wonder if Beth had caught cold from the night's chill when she returned with the empty garbage bucket and fell into a chair, her nose and cheeks blotched deep pink, her short black hair wet at the bangs and stuck to her forehead. "You all there, Betts?" Lee said. "You look right dazed." He put the teakettle on to boil. "I'm going to make you some coltsfoot tea."

"My, it's a wonderful night," Beth said, feeling breathless even though she had caught her breath. She thought of the raccoon, safe in its little wire cage. But then she jumped in her seat as if poked. "Do you think it will freeze tonight? Frost, I mean?"

"Well, it's already past mid-September," Lee said. "We could get frost any day."

"Oh, blankets. Do we have extra blankets?"

Lee came over to Beth and put a hand to her forehead. "Honey, we're not going to need extra blankets tonight." He squeezed her shoulder. "I'll keep you warm."

She took his hand and looked up into his face, ashamed at his soft smile and affectionate eyes. Here she was keeping secrets from her precious, loving Lee. But the raccoon was still out there, still chewing at its leg, probably cold without some place to hide. How could it burrow, with that trap dragging behind it like a crime?

She let Lee give her tea and bring out one of his chunkier sweaters to put around her shoulders. She tried to calm herself, curling up into a chair with her book, knowing that would please Lee. After what seemed an age but was probably only a half hour, during which Beth doodled on a blank page without really seeing what she was doing, she got up and disappeared into the bedroom. A moment later, she reemerged with the heavy sweater on and buttoned up. "I'm going to the outhouse," she said.

"You can use the indoor if you want," Lee said. They had both a real toilet and an outdoor privy, though they tried to use the indoor only in very bad weather.

"No, it's fine—I don't mind going outside." Once she was out the door, Beth ran for the compost pile again, careening left into the woods. It was almost completely dark. Just an edge of light framed the firs on the horizon, and once in the woods, Beth could barely see her own feet or anything below them. She only knew she had arrived at the cage when her shin struck it. The raccoon was silent, and very faintly in the dark, she saw the white around its black-masked face turn up to her. She unhinged the mesh of wire that served as a latch, drew an old, heavy shirt out from under her sweater, and dropped it inside the cage near the black-and-white mask. "Here, root around in this, it was my Poppa's, he sometimes gave his old clothes to the rabbits, stay warm and I'll be back tomorrow."

Back in the house, back in her chair, Beth picked up her book again, startled to see that she had drawn the beginnings of the raccoon's face, its sharp nose and long toes. She kept drawing. She was a pretty fair artist, actually. She gave the raccoon sharp teeth and an open mouth, angry and hungry. *Raccoons bark*, she wrote, *though no one ever hears them as they do this barking in private. They use their bark to make known dismay or unhappiness. It is thought that the bark resembles that of the common dog, which is why such a sound is never associated with the raccoon.*

Beth knew this wasn't true. But the idea that a world existed in which such things might be true was so delicious to her that she felt her eyes well up with tears. It would be a world only she would know. She looked up over the book at Lee, who was sitting in the old over-stuffed chair, engrossed in a magazine account of worldwide press censorship. He never looked in her book unless she showed him something. He would never know. He would think her made-up thoughts frivolous and vain. She almost smiled. Sweet Lee. Lee of the practical. She returned to her book & wrote: *Not only do raccoons bark, but earth comes up from earthwells at various points throughout the world, much the way water comes from springs. The idea of topsoil is an Indian myth, one the Indians told as a joke to the original settlers so they wouldn't find the earthwells and take control of them.*

Beth laughed out loud. When Lee jerked his head up from his reading, she said, "I'm sorry, Lee, sweetheart. I was just thinking—about, well, life on other planets."

Lee laughed without smiling. "Life on other planets! You don't believe in that claptrap, do you?"

"No," she said, laughing again at her own subterfuge. "Why do you think I'm laughing?"

The next morning, while Lee was bathing, Beth hurried out to the compost pile. The round cage was still, Poppa's shirt inside. At first Beth thought the raccoon was gone. But then she saw an edge of the trap. The raccoon was completely buried underneath the shirt, exactly as Beth had hoped. She jiggled the cage. "Hey, in there." She opened the top and dropped in cut pieces of a small apple. The mound under the shirt quivered, and puffing wet nostrils emerged from under the fabric. Beth leaned down into the cage, holding one of the segments close to the nose, though far enough away to be safe in case the coon was in a biting mood. She could see the edge of the trap at the other end of the crumpled shirt. Since the coon had to drag it wherever it went, it wouldn't be able to move fast.

But at the same instant as she saw the coon's eyes, it hissed and leaped at her hand, catching her fingers in its teeth. "Yah!" Beth screamed, jumping back from the sting that shot up her hand into her arm, curling her fingers into a fist, staring not at the coon, still snarling, but at the trap, now a good two feet away and still under Poppa's shirt. How? Then she looked back at the coon, whose rear foot was missing. Only a raw stump remained. She had heard that animals chewed off limbs frozen or diseased or caught in traps, but she thought that was a fairy-tale idea, made up to soothe children hearing the stories that animals really weren't killed and skinned after they met with hunter's traps. But it was true, and here was the hissing truth. Why hadn't she thought of it until now? Why didn't she think the raccoon would take care of itself?

The pain exploded out of her fingers after a moment of sickening numbness. Beth opened her hand; it was full of blood. The coon's teeth had stripped the skin off two fingers from middle knuckle to nail. She heard herself make an anguished sound, a groan so full of grief that hearing it saddened her, so that in the midst of her own dizzying pain, she felt sad, so sad. She sank to her knees beside the cage, holding her dripping hand. The masked face and bright eyes of the coon regarded her almost quizzically, now that she was at a distance. She tried to hate it, but she could not. It did what it had to do for itself. What any creature should.

She sat there in the leaves until the pounding in her hand wore itself down to a throb. Things loomed sharply clear around her: the rough edge of tree bark, twist and curl of dead leaf, a spider trembling on its invisible web. A woodpecker shrieked. She was unsteady when she got to her feet without help from her hands, the one hand cradling the other, but she pictured Lee's face, not as she might have seen him in the last day or so, but as when she first met him, the way he stared at her when she welcomed him to the Theosophical Society meeting as if she were an eerie light. She kept that image of his face before her as she made her way back to the house, navigating by its steadiness and intensity.

He must have seen her from the kitchen window, for by the time Beth neared the house, Lee had come out to meet her, his whole bearing a shout of worry.

"Beth, for God's sake—" He caught her hands in his two. Her fingers would scarcely pry apart for the dried blood already gluing them together. "What is it?"

"Out there—" she winced as he probed around the bite marks, seeing just how bad they were. "Back out there, an animal. My fault. Poppa's rabbits—I thought I knew something."

Lee sat her down in the grass, still morning-dewy but growing warm from the sun. "Knew what—what did you think you knew? What happened?"

"I was taking care of something—by myself. Giving food. A raccoon in a trap. I made it a little cage." She stared at him. "Lee, it chewed its leg off."

Lee had gotten a bucket of water and a piece of cloth and began daubing off the blood. "I know, honey, they do that."

"What sort of thing would chew off its leg instead of eating food?"

"Well, something in bad trouble, I suppose."

Once her hands were clean, the wounds on the two fingers looked as vivid as shoved-back skin, like badly stubbed toes. The ache made her hand thick and heavy. It was her right hand, the hand she needed to draw and write in her book. But it would heal and work again. And the book would be there. The book, that Lee had given her. How had he known she would need it so?

Lee was tying her fingers in clean cloths. "This isn't too bad. A nasty flesh wound. Though I bet it smarts plenty. Dr. Bradford two farms down can stitch you up. But Betts, honey—there's something I don't like telling you. We'll have to kill your coon to test for rabies."

"But why?"

"The rabies testers need a sample of brain tissue."

Beth didn't say anything more for a time. She saw the coon leap up and bite her again and again in her mind. What was happening around her and what she saw in her mind all merged into a blur. She let Lee put her into the little utility pushcart and with it push her down to Bradford's. Her hand hurt. Lee was right behind her the whole ride, guiding the rough cart over the stones and pits in the road, but she had never felt so alone, fogged in by the pulse of the bite under the careful bandages. There was something about being alone that way. Something private and ripe and blank. Something new and painful. It would be weeks before she could even begin to describe it, in her book, to herself.

We are leagues away from what others embrace. We have done the distance to ourselves. We look to nightfall for the raccoon's bark. We forget who we used to be. We are two together, but we are also one by one. I ride out to the earthwells and sit by them, watching. It is all right to be pregnant with the moon.

11   The Physics of Suspension

His wedding ring bit into the thick flesh of his finger. Large black shoes lined up for him in closet rows. He commanded heavy machines: table saw, lawnmower, car engine. Like scientific data, these details construct my father from precise fragments, gathered while I was growing up on the periphery of his busy structural engineer's life away from home. When he was home, outside of sporadic, awkward interventions in my discipline, my father and his concerns were the province of my mother's subtle care.

But one time after dinner when I was about twelve, when he was extravagant with wine and dizzying Los Angeles summer heat, my father said to her in front of me, "if you die before me, I wouldn't know what to do with myself." His voice trailed off, suggesting the unimaginable, the unspeakable.

"Phil, you're a fool," my mother had replied, pelting him with a balled-up cocktail napkin. I imagined the unimaginable anyway: insanity, catatonia, homelessness and mumbling. Or suicide, with one of the many guns he kept in the house, or with the car, against a wall or a freeway divider.

In fact, though, my mother was healthy, not clumsy, nor given to dangerous pastimes. She gardened. She did a lot of crossword puzzles. And she kept in phone contact with a network of friends, who often relied on her for information about one another. She was emissary at home, too; after I moved away, she and I would exchange phone calls a couple of times a month, and though my mother would always close by saying, "we love you, honey," seldom did I speak to my father directly. Once in a while he'd get on the extension and say, *How're you doing, kid?* and hang up after my one-word answer. Usually he was something on which my mother reported, like the weather, or the changing neighborhood.

Then my mother died. When I was thirty-four, in the fall, when the fire danger rating signs in the scrub-brush foothills behind their house in Los Angeles say, *Extremely High.* She liked to garden barefoot, and one day she cut an instep. The infection, initially so innocuous they didn't bother to call me, spread so quickly that it killed her. It was a nineteenth-century sort of death, one she would have marveled about had she read of it in the paper.

I was at the school in Hartford, Connecticut—where I teach disturbed ten year olds—when the school secretary took me out of class for a family call. But I thought the bad news would be about Grammy, my father's ninety-year-old mother, relegated to a nursing home in the San Fernando Valley. Grammy's death wouldn't have been the worst of news, for she suffered from what the nuns out at the Villa Probrienta called by a name as lyrical as a woman's: dementia. Grammy stole things from other patients. She wore two dresses at a time. She thought she was a girl again, a fat Austrian girl with blonde hair and strong arms. And her feces began to preoccupy her. She would collect them in a glass and leave them in other patients' rooms.

Instead of one of the nuns at Villa Probrienta that day, though, it was a nurse at my parents' community hospital. "Am I speaking with Anne Colsey?"

I chafed at my hands, smudged with colored pencil. "Yes, this is Anne. What can I do for you?" It's kind of funny to think I offered to do something for this woman, this nurse who was about to tell me my mother was dead because my father was too distraught to do it himself. When she finished telling me that she was sorry, but my mother had taken ill suddenly and had unexpectedly died, I hung up without saying anything. I stood before the phone motionless, blushing. The wood earrings my mother had given me a few years before burned in my ear-lobes. Hadn't I just spoken to her the night before? No. A week before. But she and my father were there, out in California, and they were all right. A presence I trusted like gravity, or regular paychecks. The nurse had the sense to call back and tell me again as though speaking to a child.

This time I listened. I clutched my hair with my free hand and cried, my body beginning to believe her. Dad was still staying in Mom's hospital room, where they had let him sleep during my mother's brief illness. The nurse insisted he was all right, though she did seem relieved when I told her I would come out and see that he got home. I thanked her, hung up again, and made plane reservations. I called Alan, the man I'd been seeing for several months, who listened to me cry some more and left his own job to pick me up from the school.

Then I remembered the guns my father kept, the shrug of empti-ness in his voice back down those years before and the words, *I wouldn't know what to do with myself.* My mother had neutralized those words with her jokes and her presence. But my remembering them in her absence made them real and dangerous, as if he'd just said them again, to me and to me alone.

I only remember the plane ride to Los Angeles in snapshots. It seemed people were eating a great deal. We had jolts and bumps over somewhere—mountains. The woman sitting next to me had a baby on her lap. This is what I remember best: when the mother got up to go to the toilet, she asked me if I would hold the baby. I still don't know how she knew I wanted to. There was, after all, a friendly older woman sitting on the other side of her who asked the mother about her baby. The baby, a girl, was heavy and warm.

When I got to Los Angeles, no one met me at the airport. I rented a car and drove the old shining freeways that stretched west to east, the ones I drove just to be driving when I was in my late teens. I had wanted to be moving somewhere. I wanted to be then something like where I am now: in a good job teaching in New Haven, in a large garret that I loved, on good terms with a couple of old boyfriends, and in-volved with this new one, Alan, who seemed very promising. I had wanted then to be replete, worldly, full of somewhere else. Now, it was fifteen years later. "My mother is dead," I said out loud in the car. A man grinned at me from a spectacular pink lowrider, passing me in the fast lane. The wind blowing in the window smelled like a chainsaw.

The nurses gathered around me when I arrived on my father's floor in the hospital. One of them said, "He's all right." I said, "Why did my mother die?" Two of them began to talk at once, and one went away, and I heard the words "sepsis" and "quick metabolism" and "unusual" and "advanced." Then a man appeared, and it was the doctor, and I listened very hard, but all I could think about was my mother in the garden, her back to the kitchen window, her wide hips resting on her heels, digging around, planting papery Iceland poppies and crocus that would come up a week later in the ridiculous, balmy California Decembers.

Dad was dressed and sitting on a hospital bed when I came in. One of his shoes was untied. He stood and we put our arms around each other, and I felt him shudder and press his face into my neck, making a print there with his glasses. He was warm against me like the baby on the plane. After some minutes he pulled himself away from my neck and looked at me from arm's length, tilting his head up to see me through his bifocals. His eyes were wet. "Anne, honey," he said, "let's go home."

We buried my mother at Forest Lawn on a windy, dry day. There is a space next to her for Dad, his side of the headstone smooth and speechless. I took care of flowers and cards from people. The cards praised her vibrant nature and loving heart, things you never talk about unless someone's dead. My father stood there while I answered the cards for both him and me, his hands in his pockets. "You could always say things right, Anne," he said.

I had taken family emergency leave from the school in Hartford in order to stay with him for a while after the funeral. Even though I saw him each year at Christmas, after Mom's death, everything about him seemed startling to me. Since his retirement a few years before, his thick hair had gone almost completely white. He had a telescope aimed out the porch window at the Japanese persimmon tree hung with its fat, harvest-orange persimmons. Red-shafted flickers would come to the tree and peck at the fruit.

He worked with wood in his workshop, making coasters. Sometimes he just made shapes. One day shortly after the funeral, he injured a finger when the lathe snatched the wood out of his hands and shot it at him. He came to me; I bathed the finger in too much disinfectant and swaddled it in gauze. He trimmed his beard every few days in a tiny hand mirror. He took naps curled on his side, wearing powder-blue sweat pants.

I slept, when I did sleep, in my mother's sewing room, where she had kept a small bed for her naps and most of her clothes in the closets. Each day, after hearing my father go into the bathroom, I would retrieve the paper from the driveway and put it on the breakfast table. I would make coffee and put it out next to the paper with cups and milk and sugar, the way my mother used to. Then I would wait for him, busying myself as though I was not waiting. I would do the crossword puzzle, which I hate.

Dad fell into the habit of reading the obituaries before anything else. "'Salmon, Erma P., 75. Fetch, Prescott R., 82.'" I would work on the crossword. "Dad, what's a seven-letter word for 'porous metal'?" I figured he would know the sort of manly, science-oriented words they often had in the crosswords. He would barely be listening. "Mhph. 'Steel.'"

"Not porous. Not seven letters. Come on, Dad."

"Here's a kid, just a kid, dead. 'Stevens, Ronald Kevin, 19.'"

"What's a seven-letter word for 'extreme joy'?"

"'The family requests that donations be made to the American Cancer Society. There will be no calls.'"

And so it went, through buttered toast that got cold, and jam that sat out opened and unused. I made eggs, beaten fluffy with cream. I made boxed-mix pancakes that tasted like plaster. I made pudding and Dutch babies and apple dumplings and crepes and blintzes and sausage. I tried to remember everything they used to make at the Sunday brunch in Pasadena, on the top floor of one of the fancy hotels, that my parents liked when I was a teenager. I would put on my red velvet dress and tie back my thick hair, and do my best to resemble a demure little rich girl from Pasadena. We would spoon things up with a flourish for each other, and my mother would fake a French accent.

But my father didn't eat much of the things I made, though he would always say, "Well, that looks delicious," when I set them on the table. In between reading the obituaries and looking through his telescope at the flickers, he took only small, absent bites. The circles under his eyes purpled and deepened.

About a week after the funeral he put away his telescope, even though there was still plenty of fruit on the tree and the flickers were still coming. He did it before I awoke, so it wasn't until midafternoon that I sensed the kitchen was missing something. "Dad?" I called, overloud in the small house. "Dad, there're cedar waxwings out on the tree. Aren't they kind of rare here?" Still no response. "Dad?" I called through the house, over and over.

I finally found him in his workshop, a small outbuilding at the edge of the property, where he was covering the lathe and the belt sander and the table saw.. "What are you doing, Dad?" I said. "Don't you need to do some more shapes or coasters or something?"

He turned his head over his shoulder at me, but his eyes didn't meet mine. He waved a hand at the room full of things. "What useless shit." It sounded like the speech of a profane stranger. Behind him was a wall of little plastic drawers, each of which held a tiny handful of variously sized nails and screws and wingnuts. There was a deep freezer full of meat he won in an office drawing before retiring. There were old toasters. I thought of my tiny apartment in Hartford, which I had stocked with the smallest version of all household essentials for space-saving's sake. Except I had two huge cutting boards, made for me as a gift by one of my aides at the school.

"Dad," I said, moving around in front of him, taking hold of one end of the saw cover, as if to tug it from him, to keep him from covering up the machines. "Dad, I need—a cutting board. Make me a cutting board. Please?"

He released the cover, and his end of it slapped against my knees. "Why don't you just buy yourself one," he said, moving away from me and out the door, his soft loafers swallowing the pat of his footsteps. I covered the saw myself, the jagged teeth on its round blade unbearably cruel.

Then I went back to the house and sat down in the living room. I took up a magazine, *Good Housekeeping,* its address label bearing my mother's name. Dad was out of sight in the kitchen. He sniffed. A cabinet door squeaked. The magazine glared up from my lap, its cover making lavish promises for recipes, for clever crafts.

I heard my father's voice from the kitchen, low and tense. "What is it with this?" I went out there to find him trying to mix himself a glass of chocolate milk. But the chocolate powder wasn't dissolving. He had spooned out powdered baking cocoa instead of the pre-sugared Quik mix with the cheerful cartoon faces on the label. How could someone this helpless be my father?

"Jesus, Dad, weren't you an engineer all those years?"

He studied the labels on the two chocolate powders I put before him. "I never had to design a glass of chocolate milk," he said.

"Well, you better start paying attention, man." I sounded like one of my more messed-up ten year olds, whose constant battles for self-control made them grittier and more candid than other children. "Mom's not around to wait on you hand and foot anymore."

As soon as the words were out of my mouth I regretted them, though I kept standing there with my arms folded. The posture I used to take with Mom when she and I quarreled. He froze, fists leaning on the counter. He then stood straight and faced me. "I am your father, Anne."

I held Dad's stare. I was ten years old again and wanted to break things. At sixteen: Dad grounded me. He stood in the driveway to keep me from leaving with the car. When I was nineteen: Dad had an ulcer and for a long time no one knew. He was furious with pain at everyone. He threw a glass of water at me across the room for a snotty remark I made to my mother. It all happened again in a rude collision as I stood before him with the words vibrating between us. *I am your father, Anne.*

But it wasn't the same, and he wasn't the father he had been before, because everything was different now, because my mother wasn't there and wouldn't be there. There was no Anne and there was no Dad.

There were just these people standing in a Southern California kitchen, a glass of bitter chocolate milk between them. "Yes, you are my father," I said to him. I made him a glass of proper chocolate milk.

I went back to my room, my mother's room, closed the door and looked at my clothes, hanging in the closet where I'd cleared a space in the bank of my mother's clothes. I read my address book. There were exactly twenty names. I called my answering machine back in Hartford. I had five messages: two from Alan, two from friends checking in to see how I was, and one from the superintendent of the school, who said things were going fine and there was no rush of course but could I call sometime and let them know when I might be coming back? I had the front section of yesterday's newspaper on the bed, full of unchangeable news. I weighed myself. My mother always kept the scale in her room, saying a woman's weight had a right to its privacy. Then I took all my clothes off and weighed myself again.

I lay down on the bed naked. When you are born, you aren't quite naked, but have the caul on you, or your mother's blood, and then a lot of hands touch you and wipe your mother's stain away. Then you grow up, wearing clothes your parents buy for you. Later, when you are with men, or with women, you still aren't really naked, for they cover you with themselves. I lay on my mother's bed, and the dry, dry breeze came in the window. My skin was dry and bare, like old bone. I would never see my mother again. There were only the tricks of her smell and her clothing and her things around me. I curled myself together into a ball. I did not weep—tears are easy, so right at funerals, where their choke and squeeze offer a kind of pleasure. I took the truth and finality of my nakedness without her somewhere unseen, inside the body where all the organs are dark. I clutched my own legs so hard that later my shoulders were sore. I stayed like that for a time. Then I met something like sleep.

When I awoke, I had been covered with a fleece blanket that smelled of cedar. It was nearly dark outside, the relief of the west hills edged in pale gold light. I dressed and went out in search of my father, through the hall where my mother's feet had packed the carpet down. The house was dark, but there was light coming from the den where the heavy chest of drawers stood.

Dad was sitting on the floor with his antique shotgun across his lap, its felt wrapper laid open around it like gift paper. He was holding a handgun, a World War II Lueger pistol, one of his favorites. From time to time as I was growing up, he would sit out there this way, polishing or just admiring the weapons. They were so shiny they looked wet.

I stopped and stood there in front of him. "What are you doing?" I said.

"Just looking at old things," he said. A vision played, of him raising the shotgun to his shoulder and pointing it at me, pointing at himself, awkwardly. It wasn't real. It had never happened. But the mind—the mind is a frightened child, seeing monsters everywhere. Or a genie, taunting you with three wishes. I wanted for it to bring my mother back, her hand on Dad's shoulder, her print dress like a painting against the dark wood of the living room. It obeyed. I saw her for an instant. And then there was just Dad again, now looking up at me, his face the pale orb of a stranger's.

"I've been thinking," I said, my throat dry and sore, as if I'd been screaming. "I've been thinking that maybe you should come live with me, you know, come be roommates with me for a while." Actually I had been thinking nothing of the kind. I was wondering what to do now. I could not go back to Hartford and leave my father to his nest of guns, to his drawers full of keys to cars that could go a hundred miles an hour. But I could not stay.

"Live with you?" he said. The hopeful sound of it lit up his face for a moment, and in his innocent interest, I suddenly saw him very old, like Grammy in the nursing home, cheerful at anyone's entrance because no one in particular mattered anymore.

"For a while," I said. "You know." The hopeful tethers holding his face near a smile collapsed, and he shook his head.

"Oh, Dad," I said, but I could not fix it, could not promise to be there with the perfect recipe, like *Good Housekeeping*.

"I belong with your mother. That's where I've always been."

"But you can't go where she is now."

He considered that. "Well, then I belong where she was." He looked around the room. "Here."

I was not looking at the guns in his lap but seeing them anyway. I wanted to ask him about them, about the dark parts of the house, about the pictures on the walls that Mom had liked and the fabric furniture whose pattern had been her choosing. I wanted to ask him who would send me my birthday cards and say *we love you, honey*, at the end of every phone call. Who would report on him to me, as on the weather, or the changing neighborhood.

"But do you know what you're going to do with yourself?"

He folded the felt wrap back over the guns. "No," he said, putting them back into their drawers. He looked for a few moments at the closed drawer, a sigh whistling out of his throat. Then he held out a hand to me from his cross-legged position on the floor. "But I know what you're going to do right now. You're going to help me up." I took one of his meaty hands in my two and jerked him to his feet. He held his head up so as to frame my face in his bifocals. His dark eyes were huge and damp. "Do you want to take a walk?" he said. "Your mother and I used to walk, about this time."

We put on walking shoes, in our separate bedrooms, and met in the front hallway. The evening sky was purple and close, and the air smoky with the millions of cars that had passed through it all day long, all over Los Angeles. Dad took my hand and ran it through his arm, and we walked like that, like an elderly courting couple, for a silent mile or two, around darkening, quiet residential streets and driveways full of cars. I hadn't touched him so continuously since when I was very small and, sensing the remoteness by which I would come to know him, I would conquer his lap and demand his attention for a childish accomplishment or difficulty. It was strange, walking so with one's father, but then, everything between us now was strange, and new, and impossible. His whole life seemed an undiscovered country.

When we approached home, I drew my hand away. "It would be nice to walk somewhere every night," I said. "You should do that. Will you do that? And call me about it, and tell me where you've been?"

"I could," he said. "Do you walk back in Connecticut?"

"Sometimes. When it's not too cold." Actually I never did—I worked out inside a big noisy YMCA, an oddity in comparison with the dusty tangerine trees and jade bushes and silent suburban homes all over my parents' neighborhood.

"Will you go back there soon?" he asked.

"I think so," I said. "Maybe by next week. They're missing me. The ten year olds, I mean."

"Good," he said. "It's good that you belong somewhere. You're a good kid, Annie." It was sweet, and he was smiling, but he sounded like he was talking to a teenager, to some Anne I hadn't been for a while. To him I was probably still the foolish mystery all teenagers are to their parents. He had spent his days then pondering the physics of suspension, not the touchy, girl-oriented problems of his only child. He'd never had to notice that my concerns spread out toward the rest of life, toward experiences that overlapped his own.

"Dad," I said, and then stopped. The dark driveway pooled before us. "I can't believe what we've lost," I said at last.

He put his hand on my neck and chafed the skin there. His rough fingers hurt. "I miss her, too," he said. "Miss her in everything." He cleared his throat, looking around at the shadows of bottlebrush and ivy framing the driveway as though he might find something comforting in them.

But that wasn't what I meant at all. I was thinking suddenly about the years of emptiness between him and me, put there by my dead mother, who in her desire to be everything to us, had kept each of us to herself. "You know, Mom loved you," I said. "And she loved me." I put my hand over his on my neck and tried to see him in the dark. "I'm not sure that was always good. I mean, loving—loving, you know, isn't—sometimes, loving is for yourself. It's selfish. Sometimes love is like that. Do you see?"

"Selfish?" He took his hand away. "No—I don't see. Whatever could you mean?"

"I'm not sure, I guess." The air around us was thick with the nervous trilling of crickets and katydids, and the distant surf of the Glendale-Ventura Freeway interchange five miles away. "You used to build bridges," I said. "You used to build bridges, and that's about all I ever knew about you."

"I'm not doing that anymore."

"I know that. But I don't know what else you do, really. All I ever knew was what Mom told me. You never tell me." My throat filled for the hundredth time that week with stupid tears. Would I never exhaust them?

"So ask," he said, very low.

"Okay," I said. "Okay, I'll ask. I will." Still, I could not ask then, which was the likely thing to do, since I'd wanted it, and had been invited. Tomorrow—then I would start. It would be a task for the years, this knowing of my father, this recognition of him by more than bits and pieces. But I did not want to begin exchanging my mother for him—not just yet. I was somewhere in between knowing either of them, somewhere suspended in the soft, numbing night. For the moment, at least, his voice in the dark was all I could stand. And with the echo of it leading me to him, I followed him inside, up the front steps, under the porch light's glow.

Part IV

Home

12 Flight

When his doctors insisted that at seventy-six he was too deaf to drive anymore, Johannes Mulzit took up beekeeping. He was not clumsy, nor forgetful. He could still drive just yards behind the car in front of him like everyone else on the Los Angeles freeways. He still remembered that the drive to Redondo pier, where he went fishing twice a week, required twenty minutes on the Harbor Freeway and then a right turn at Sepulveda Boulevard.

So too did Johannes remember what he read in the mail advertisement entitled *Beekeeping at Home*—a vividly colored pamphlet that ordinarily he would have discarded along with ads for correspondence courses and for winning Hawaiian vacations. He had been fascinated by the close-up photos of bees, clustered around the shelter of their hive. Later, having read the books about bees from the library, Johannes remembered that bees need air and warmth and a steady source of energy, the way fire does. He remembered that they needed to be kept clean. And then his hands were steady and purposeful when he put them, naked before the hundreds of sheathed stingers on smoke-drunk bees, inside the housing boxes from which he drew the bees' first honeycombs for inspection.

Yet Johannes could not deny his difficulty with cars. He had met with his third accident only a week before the doctor's pronouncement, again because he could not hear a vehicle's approach, this time the back-up beeper on a truck in a parking lot. At first he could not believe that he was losing his hearing, for he still heard sounds in his ears. But the sounds he heard and the world he saw around him did not always correspond anymore. He began to remember the voices of his younger life more clearly—those of his father and mother, of his brother, of former employers, of people whom he had not seen in years. It was pleasant in a way, but one could not tell of this pleasure to anyone, least of all to a policeman, after a collision with another car, however minor.

His wife never learned to drive. Johannes could not imagine it and had never taught her. His son, Willy, grown up and too tall for Johannes's comfort, offered to do whatever driving was necessary and arranged for delivery people to bring in food every week. Buses went everywhere, even though in Johannes's estimation they were too full of strangers and too slow. But there was no help for it, the audiologist declared: for the rest of his days, for Johannes to travel meant relying on the bus or his own feet or the willingness of others. He could not fly about in the car on the freeways as easily and as often as he once had.

Teresa Mulzit had never grown used to her husband's tendency to disappear in the car for hours at a time, but neither did she appreciate his desire for bees. "Why can you not make rabbits, the way we did in Austria?" she said after she overheard Johannes telling Willy, at lunch one day, of his plans to start the bee colony. She was thinking of sixty years earlier, when they both were teenagers on their families' farms in rural Austria.

Willy watched his mother speak as though her question held great import. He came to lunch every week, and ate with Johannes in the high-ceilinged kitchen of their great shabby Victorian house. Teresa stood and served the men their soup and chicken legs and then took the plates away; she would eat alone later, after Willy had gone back to his office and Johannes vanished into the house's depths or out into the concrete yard, or into the garage that held his saws and tools. "We can eat the rabbits, save money on buying chicken like this here," she continued.

"Ah, you shut up," Johannes said to his wife, as he often did, though his voice held no rancor. It was as though he had worn out the phrase from frequent use. "You don't know what the hell you're talking about." He hadn't fully heard what she said, but he recognized the meaning of her tight frown and caught the words "not," "rabbits," "save."

"*Ja*, sure, bees can kill you," Teresa said. "I heard it on the TV. They come up from Africa and take over from the good bees."

Johannes glared at his food. Willy held up his fork. "Mutti, that threat's overrated," he said, loudly enough for someone outside to hear. "Supposedly the strain of aggressive bees is interbreeding with the more docile ones." Willy was an arbitration lawyer. He chewed his chicken carefully, sipped his soup without a sound. "It might be good for Poppa to have bees. He can put the boxes against the fence by the old playground."

That location was the best in the yard for such an enterprise; in fact, Johannes had already thought of it himself. It was well away from the apartment where their Mexican tenants lived, and from the garage and the empty apartment above it that they were trying to rent. He considered his son at the table, his fine features and smooth, short hair. Skin smooth as a woman's. Willy was a smart boy, his teachers had always said, though he never could drive a nail very well or run a saw.

"Nah, that's too close to the house," Johannes said. He pushed his plate away so sharply the silverware on it slipped to the table with a clatter. "I got a better place." He hadn't a better place until just that moment, but it was so good a place that he was surprised he hadn't thought it up years ago, savoring its cleverness for a just such a day as this.

Teresa and Willy waited. Johannes said nothing. He didn't have to tell them all the time where he was going to be and what he was going to do. For years, in addition to his fishing trips to the beach, he frequented the junkyard in search of parts for his various carpentry jobs, had beers in bars he knew and some he didn't, or just drove the freeways when he had no particular place to be. His El Camino was old and dented and its bed in back full of sacked painting rags and scrap wood, but its engine was as muscular as the newer cars were meek and economical. In it Johannes covered thousands of Southern California miles, sharp smoggy wind or softer ocean air rushing in the window. On a whim he could drive the Santa Monica Freeway west to the San Diego north, then run with the Ventura east to the Golden State south, which curved back into the Santa Monica toward West 18th Street again, and in doing so trace a whole square of world around where he lived in a matter of hours.

Johannes would forget the day of the week, the hour, on such excursions. His foot on the accelerator became an invisible working part of the car itself. When he was a boy in Austria, men occasionally walked the perimeter of their farmlands. Johannes would never own big open land such as that, never claim any legal title to the asphalt-covered acreage described by his travels, but the places bounded by those freeways belonged to him anyway, because he knew them, knew their rough smells and neighborhood noises and constant surge of human activity. There was a liquor store covered with iron bars run by a lone woman and her dog with one eye on Crenshaw Boulevard, where Johannes sometimes stopped and bought a German-language newspaper. There was a huge wig warehouse on Olympic with a fifty-foot woman's head of hair painted on a wall visible from the freeway. Through the Santa Monica Mountains the San Diego cut a swath like a rude gray river, west of the foolish splendor of Beverly Hills and Bel Air. His domain had a thousand faces: the endless dead in Forest Lawn, the scrubby bluffs of Griffith Park, the lowrider specialty shops in Echo Park—there were three on the same block.

"Well, Poppa," said Willy. "What's your better place?" Teresa lingered at his elbow, taking longer than necessary to clear his dishes. Johannes thought he could feel their breathing in his face. He hadn't forgotten the doctor's ban on driving. But his new sanctuary didn't require a car. It was the vast, rolling roof of the sewing machine factory next door, whose three-story brick wall faced one side of the Mulzits' courtyard. A person could get up there easily—up the wood-frame staircase to the empty apartment above the garage, onto the cinderblock wall supporting the staircase, then up the short ladder clinging to the brick wall next to the apartment. Once on the red-tiled roof all one could see were its humps and valleys and its squat silver ventilators. Johannes had once beaten Willy for going on this roof, as the sewing machine factory had declared it illegal to trespass there. But it would be a perfect place for Johannes to put his bees. From the roof he could see in every direction and watch the cars go by on the freeway.

"It's someplace," he said, though instead of sounding elusive, he sounded childish. He cleared his throat and stood up. "I got to work and get it ready."

"Poppa," Willy said, slow and loud. "You have to tell us where it is. You're not going to drive anywhere, are you?"

"Huh?" Johannes said, not waiting for the answer. Teresa's and Willy's voices blurred to a murmur behind him as he went down the hall toward the stairs. He visited the folded cash supply he kept hidden in a toilet paper roll high in the medicine chest; he would have banks no more than necessary. When he came downstairs with his hat on, Willy met him at the front door, followed by Teresa. "Poppa, I hate to say this, but if you're going to drive, I will have to take your keys away and maybe even the car."

Willy didn't look like he hated saying it, Johannes thought. He squinted at Willy, the way he had at his son's boyhood misbehaviors. The caution still rose in Willy's face. *You do like I tell you,* Johannes heard his own father say in his mind, from sixty-five years before. *You paddle fast when you try going upstream.* He and his father were fishing on a makeshift raft. Johannes was young and not yet strong.

"I don't drive," Johannes said, loud and slow as if it was Willy who had trouble hearing. "I don't hear so good no more. I go on the bus."

"But where you go?" said Teresa.

"I go get the bees."

Even though they had the biggest pet store in Southern California, the people in Downey could only give Johannes addresses and phone numbers for bee shipping companies, and send him to the library for educational books. It was not like buying an aquarium, which one could purchase and set up in an afternoon. One had to learn about supers and queen excluders and smokers and the Langstroth design, which required that hive construction always allow bees 5/16th of an inch of workroom, no more and no less. One had to order a starter package of bees with a queen inside, which came through the mail like clothing or pears at Christmas. One could discern the mood of the bees by the quality of their collective hum. Johannes read his library books as though he were interpreting ancient texts. He wrote the German words in faint pencil over English ones he couldn't understand.

He shouted Teresa away from the garage workshop where he read the books, and where he assembled the boxes from the factory, delivered by a puzzled postal worker. He ignored the books on rabbitry she had Willy buy and leave lying around the house. The beekeeping equipment was more costly than he had expected, so he raised by five dollars the monthly rent of the Mexican tenants in the apartment and the Chinese boy down the hall in their big house. This was all right, he decided, since he would give them some honey when it was ready. He finished assembling the parts to the hive just days before the bees came, delivered by the same perplexed postal worker.

But first there was the problem of getting the hive onto the roof. Johannes saved the final building and painting of the hive until after he transported all its parts onto the roof, a task that he undertook at night with the aid of the tiny but powerful flashlight Willy had given him one Christmas. When Teresa's faint breaths told Johannes that she was asleep in the twin bed next to him, he slipped down the stairs and outside to the workshop, where he gathered the hive pieces together and made a pile of them on the landing at the top of the apartment stairs. There he tied the hive pieces to his back with cast-off clothing torn into thick strips. Then, his flashlight between his teeth, he climbed the stairs and then the ladder, untying the sash and leaving the piece behind before going back to the stair landing for another piece.

With all the hive pieces finally on the roof, Johannes lay down on the rough tile, still warm from the last sun hours before. There were still cars hissing by on the freeway—there were always cars, even at one in the morning. Their gathering roar and retreating moans penetrated Johannes's failing ears. Only a few stars peered down from the dark sky, edged in pink by a million amber streetlights. The night air around him tasted like dust. A freeway billboard bathed in light pictured joyous people drinking canned beer & wine.

The movement of the cars reminded Johannes of the rush of water, the waters of rivers that flowed by him when he was a boy back in Austria. How much water had flowed by him that he hadn't even noticed? Where had it gone? Into the sea a thousand miles away from his boyhood town. Years of his life into the mouths of fishes. He heard laughter. Quickly, he sat up and looked around, but no one was there. It was the laughter of his brother—he knew it from its brash loudness. He smiled at it in the dark. His foolish brother Karl, lanky and loud and afraid of nothing. Dead now of some cancer—dead for twenty years, but still laughing like a young boy in his brother's old mind.

After a long time Johannes descended the ladder and went back to bed, practicing the smooth, definite movements his books said would reassure his bees. He knew he was being quiet, even though he could not hear it. He heard ringing, and cheering, and the hum of the bees he did not yet own. The bedroom where Teresa lay was dark, deep as a dream; he felt fond of her, lying in her bed trusting the darkness.

But when he lay down, and the pressure of his own ears' noises stilled along with his breathing, he heard Teresa begin to curse him in German, then in English, then in German and English colliding. "*Ich haß dich,* you pig, you fool, you lover of filth, *dein Mutter war eine Teufelin,* you shame yourself and your father and everyone you have ever known, *du frißt wie ein Schwein, du bist ein schrecklicher Säufer,* you are only a wretch among men." Her voice was even and clear, listing his sins over the years—his stinginess with her, his extravagance with his friends, his carelessness, his drunkenness, his hands on her in anger, on their son, the times he did not pay for things he should have, the women they sometimes encountered whom only he seemed to know well.

His wife had never spoken so to him. She was a good wife that way, most of the time. But this voice in the dark—he did not know it. He lay there in silence until it stopped. Then he fell asleep, trembling. In the morning he saw his wife in her dressing gown arranging her hair. The words in the dark, however true, were never discussed. Teresa did not treat him any differently. Perhaps only his mind had heard the curses for him—he wanted to ask her. But he did not.

By the time the bees arrived, the hive was assembled on the roof, its pale yellow paint dry at last. Johannes had built a shade shelter for it, since the books had warned against extreme temperatures. It was Los Angeles, after all, whose summer heat could suck away sweat as soon as it wet the skin. Bees enjoy order and control and temperatures of 93 degrees Fahrenheit inside their brood chambers. Too hot and wax melts, honey runs.

It was beautiful, this towering hive, its proud metal roof level with Johannes's chest. It was full of potential, the kind a man feels on arriving in a new place with his errors behind him. Johannes didn't know when he had beheld a thing so pure. He wanted to live in it himself, to work among the many workers that would soon be there, who didn't hear any better than he did—bees rely on smell for information, not on their hearing. Johannes thought he could still smell things pretty well. He snuffled the air more carefully now, in partnership with his bees to come.

The bees arrived, vibrating in their plain shipping box. By this point, Teresa had figured out where he had installed the hive and told Willy. In the late afternoon of the day the bees arrived, they both watched Johannes mount the stairs and scale the wall, and then vanish with the bee box over the top of the ladder. "Well, at least the only neck he'll break will be his own," Willy said.

"Can you not stop him?" Teresa pulled on her son's arm. "He's a crazy man. He will fall from up there!"

"Look, Mutti, leave him alone, okay? He'll be all right." Willy kept looking at where the roof's edge met the pale blue sky.

"I do not know what to think," Teresa said, almost to herself. "People will say, there is the wife of the crazy one. They will say that I made him crazy!" She stared up at Willy, as though he had accused her. "You marry some man, you wind up with a different one." She waved at the roof. "You wind up with some crazy man!"

"Come on," said Willy, pulling her toward the back door. "Ignore him. It'll make him wonder. Go work on something outside. Smile at him nice when he comes down. He'll think you're nuts, too."

*

The first weeks went just the way the books said. The bees settled into their box, and came and went like little machines. Johannes could not hear their sounds well, but he learned to read his bees' moods by placing his hands on the sides of their box. Low vibration indicated contented productivity. Their odors began to speak to him. Sweet rich smells like baking cake meant happy bees, but a smell like bananas rose up after one of the bees stung something. They seemed inclined to sting his dark leather boots. Johannes puffed smoke from his smoker then, smoking the banana smell away so it would not alarm the other bees. Not one of his bees had stung him, not even when he first brought them to their hive, when most clumsy beginners get their first stings.

He lost interest in his other projects, even necessary ones like fixing the plumbing in the big house when the Chinese boy's bathtub clogged up, or replacing the ragged screens in the Mexicans' apartment. He became braver about going on the roof during the daytime and took a lawn chair up to the roof to watch his bees come and go. He got some red watercolor paint one day and daubed it on a few dozen bees, and waited for them to come back—it took them about two hours. He painted his hand all over with sugar-water and let the bees lick his sweet skin. He wondered if this was how a mother feels about her children. He was a father, but it was different being a father. A father was someone who saw to his child's righteousness. A father let the world teach his child its lessons, and sometimes he was the agent of those lessons with his strong hand on the belt.

But these little bees! Johannes wanted to protect them, to touch them and feel them touching him, to know their need of him, of his ministrations against disease and invaders. And they seemed to be grateful—still he went unstung. Their whirrings around his face when he approached were curious, never aggressive. They tumbled over his fingers when he shook them from their frames. They inspected the cuffs of his shirts as if enjoying the color and design. He dreamed of them at night. He planted more flowers in the yard.

But other tasks needed doing, and finally there was really no more important work to do on the bees until later in the summer when he could begin harvesting honey. So days went by, then a week, then two, in which Johannes fixed plumbing in the house, repaired wiring, hammered nails squeezing up from floorboards, even fixed Teresa's creaky built-in ironing board without being asked. He reread his bee books at night in his living room chair, the television only a cackle through the murk of his feeble ears. But he did not care so much about the hearing problem, or what he might be missing without his car to move around in. His bees were moving for him. Besides, he could still do all the moving around he wanted to—he could go up to his bees, he could read books, and he could make it to the dinner table at night.

When he returned to the bees, they were gone.

The hive stood there, as sturdy and erect as ever, but only a few bees meandered around the shelf opening. When Johannes opened up all the boxes, he could see the burst peanut-shaped swarm cells—if only he had come earlier and seen them before! There were some brood cells left, and a few bees, but scarcely enough to recover from the enormous swarm that gathered itself up and left in his absence. There wasn't enough honey to bother harvesting. He couldn't even see a queen, without whom the colony could not live. But he had protected them! They were not overcrowded; they were not without air. Why did they go? Where did they go? How could they have vanished into the endless miles of Los Angeles without him?

A shrill breeze whipped at Johannes's back from the west, from the pier at Santa Monica where he used to go fishing. He knew how to get there without thinking—on to the Harbor Freeway for just a mile, a sharp right at the Santa Monica, straight west past the fickle Century City skyline, changing constantly with new high-rises and corporate plazas. Yet from the moving vantage of a car on the freeway, city change seemed natural, like seasonal weather patterns. One moved and the city moved too.

This was right. Even bees move. Swarming is what they do when they want to go somewhere else. It happens. But why now, and why to Johannes, when he had done everything he could to keep his bees in place with him on West 18th Street? He beat a fist down on the top of the hive, and the few confused bees remaining swirled in the air, aimlessly.

But finally, Johannes thought, what is unnatural is not moving. His bees had just done what they know how to do, what they can do. It was not their fault. He was the frozen one, the helpless one, the one who couldn't hear and couldn't drive. Without his ears, without his car, Johannes thought he might as well be a streetlight, or a building, or a senseless statue. Everything roared and swarmed beyond him, and without him. He was a part of nothing alive if he could not move.

To hell with this, Johannes whispered to no one. He scrambled back down the ladder, nearly slipping in his haste. He ran down the stairs by the empty apartment, as quickly as his old knees would allow. The keys to the El Camino were deep in a kitchen drawer full of knives and prickly rasps. Teresa was at the sink and jumped when he burst in, and he just barely heard her shriek his name as he wheeled and rushed down the back door steps. Months had passed since it had been started, but the El Camino rumbled and kicked over, and he backed unsteadily out of the long driveway. Once in the street, the car leaped forward when he shoved his foot down on the accelerator.

He did not know where to look for them, though the bees' plaintive humming seemed to throb in his head, as though they were lost and in need of him. He drove to the plot of grass three blocks away that served the neighborhood children as a football field and searched all the trees for the dark drooping cluster that swarming bees would form outside of a hive. He drove up and down the streets of the better houses, looking in their orange trees, hydrangeas, and bougainvillea. He checked each tall streetlight. Sometimes drivers in other cars passed him with angry looks, as Johannes rolled slowly along street after street.

One driver in a white Mercedes gave a shrill honk at the El Camino's sudden stop, when something like a heavy blob caught Johannes's eye in a backyard walnut tree. He hastily double-parked the car and hurried across the street to the chain-link fence isolating the tree and the smooth lawn beneath it, and then he lifted the gate latch and went inside. The bees were a fury inside his head. They had to be there—of course they were there. They were singing to him, begging him to take them home. He looked up, trying to see them in the tree.

But then there was the *hey, hey, hey* of a big dog barking that he saw before he heard in the next door yard, and a rough shake of his shoulder, and a tall, heavy woman with a rake who appeared before him when he turned around. *What the hell are you doing back here? Huh? Huh?* came dimly down the long corridor of his hearing, and he did not answer, but pointed at the walnut tree, thickly green and leafy, at its center, where a shadow played, only a shadow, not the clump of bees he hoped he would find. And then he wondered, as if the thought had been chasing him and only just caught up, what would he have done if the bees had been there?

And there was the big woman, her long hair slicked back tight in a rubber band, her face flushed and round and her mouth full of teeth, her rake poised, as ready to bite him as the dog still rhythmically barking behind the fence next door. It was like seeing the woman on Crenshaw who sometimes gave him pipe tobacco for free, except it wasn't, because this woman might hurt him, and could, and she was taller than he was and heavy, and even her bare knees were red and angry.

"Are you crazy, old man?" she said, but he did not answer. He ran to the gate like a boy to his mother. "I should call the cops!" she yelled after him, but he did not stop. The El Camino was still running—he hadn't even shut off the ignition, a foolish error in the city. But it was there, and he got in fast, turning the key before remembering that he didn't need to. He winced at the sharp shriek from the grinding starter, put the car in gear and drove away. A few blocks away, a police car passed him going the other direction, and for a moment Johannes was afraid. He watched the police car disappear in his rearview mirror. It did not matter anyway. No one would put an old man in prison for going into a back yard, but Willy would now have good reason to take the keys and the El Camino from Johannes at last. His cocky, grown-up son! The only reason Willy knew how to drive at all was because he, Johannes, had sat with Willy when he was a wriggling teenager and shown him how, over and over.

Johannes pulled over to a curb and stopped. The car thrummed beneath him, though he could only feel it. He did hear voices, dim conversations happening without him, as if he were passing slowly through a crowd and hearing only pieces of sentences and replies: *Do you think?* and *the time seems right for it* and *water temperatures change* and *best thing I ever saw.* He heard the tall woman with the rake: *What the hell! What the hell!* He looked around, though he knew no one would be there. No one was. He was hearing everything he had ever heard—all those words had gotten in his mind and were banging around like bugs in a box.

His bees were gone for good. He had blundered into someone's backyard, dreaming he could get them back. What a fool he was! In front of the whole world, no less. It took him a minute to remember where he lived, and another minute to remember how to get there. He drove home as quickly as he dared, wanting to get out of the car as soon as possible, away from its familiar embrace. Right then he only wanted the touch of things he knew he could have, that would not fly away or get taken away or escape. Usually it was cars that broke down, their parts wearing out and rattling together. But this car, this old betrayer—it had outlasted him. It would go to someone else now, someone who would take it places he would not know, for whom its engine would run without complaint. It was not particular, after all. It did not need him to keep moving. It belonged to no one. Johannes left the car by the curb in front of the house and slipped its keys in the candy dish in the parlor. The keys' gold-and-silver-colored metal gleamed there like the wrappers on the sourballs, together a shiny offering to any passerby.

Teresa was weeping at the kitchen table when he came in. She had twisted a kitchen towel into a thin rope and was pressing it hard against her forehead. When she saw him, she moaned. As he stood there, she came over and put her arms around him, and then pushed him away as if the touch of him pained her. "Why you come back," she said. "Why not just go kill yourself. Then I know where you are anyway."

He watched her as she sat back down at the table. He wanted to tell her about the woman with her angry rake and the terrible barking dog and the dark clump in the walnut tree that was nothing at all. But he could not. "Did you curse at me one night?" he said. "Did you say one night I was shameful? Not too long ago."

She moaned again. "What you are talking about? But it is true. You are shameful to drive when you could kill somebody, and have those bees, and make worry for everyone—"

But Johannes didn't try to hear the rest. He approached his wife and watched her mouth move, looked at her eyes, her paling hair. He even thought he could smell her—she often wore the citrusy German powder that women everywhere seemed to like, sent from Vienna by her sister. The kitchen table was narrow. He reached across it, picked up her arm, and put his nose to it. The skin there had something of the powdery scents from all the women he had ever been near, and their voices came together in a whir inside his ears, so loud that for a moment he thought they might appear before him in a crowd.

"Teresa," he said, though he hardly heard himself say it. But her mouth stopped moving, and it was she alone who faced him, her own particular scent mingling with and rising above the powder. Bees might meet millions of other bees as they roamed the world, and even get confused and lost, but one way they got home was by knowing its smell. It was a way a man could know home, Johannes thought, if he couldn't figure it out any other way. Though, too, there was the frail heft of Teresa's arm still in his hand, the kitchen with its dingy walls and familiar light, and the haven of the house itself, on top of the third of an acre whose deed bore their names. Amid this welter of things that never moved, across the kitchen table from his wife, Johannes sat himself softly down.

13 The House on Figueroa

The day the man came about taking her house away, Mrs. Teresa Mulzit preached again on the nature of smog. *"Ja,* now see, there is the smog everywhere but here," she said. She pointed at the dark haze on what horizon was visible through clustered buildings. "There, and there, and there. You see the brown, *ja?* But not here." She put her hand in front of her face.

Standing before her was Luz Padrilla, her tenant from the house next door. Luz nodded yes—she had heard this before—but she swayed from side to side so that the thick black braid down her back said no, this way and that. Mrs. Mulzit continued, "We are extra lucky here. The wind comes from the ocean, keeps the smog away." Luz considered old white women's ways, how the more clouded and milky their blue eyes become, the more they claim to know everything. It was all right for Luz to say, "Hm, well, Mrs. Mulzit, it may be so," as long as the braid down her back could tell the truth.

The night before, Luz had sat up late, watching. The sky never got dark, as usual. She listened for the moments when no cars passed on the freeways fencing them on all sides, and when it was quiet, she would hold her breath, and be quiet too, making the instant of quiet her own. Something would be different after this, she was sure. She felt a hint of it in her body, a special ache and heaviness as when she carried her children, a feeling which does not lie. Finally about four, when Luz was nearing sleep, she heard brisk footsteps down the sidewalk, right under her bedroom window. Someone walked along in crisp shoes and whistled as he went, whistling as if his heart were very light. Happiness without reason meant change, as sure as clouds meant weather. Luz resolved to clean tomorrow and weed the garden in order to be ready.

Ed Thorns, the man who came about Mrs. Mulzit's house, lived in Pasadena with his wife and two children. He loved his family very much, and he believed in his love for them—the way he believed in the restorative power of travel and the efficacy of antibiotics. He missed the turnoff for West 18th Street from the Harbor Freeway three times. When he finally caught the off-ramp its abruptness astonished him. Its angle would be hard to negotiate on a bicycle; his white Toyota strained. Innocent engineers in the 1930s had built the ramp for big, slow Pontiacs and Studebakers.

The big Victorian house loomed at him, dark over the several tenements and sausage factory on the brief block of West 18th Street. Ed felt a glimmer of fear, as if he'd startled something watching him. But his was a cheerful errand. The city historical society had sent him to offer Mrs. Mulzit a handsome sum for her house. They wanted to take the house away and make it a historical monument. It would become an office for lawyers and bear a plaque for people to read. Mrs. Mulzit would become a rich woman. Everyone would be happy: the historical society, along with the city and developers who wanted the entire block of West 18th Street for a car dealership; and Mrs. Mulzit, who could live anywhere else she wanted. Ed Thorns whistled to himself while driving downtown for this task.

Gina Francielli was drawing in her cleavage that morning with the cheap light lipstick she had bought just for that purpose. You just shade around the curve of the bosom a bit, the women's magazines said, and you will look more romantic. Gina lived in the apartment across the courtyard from the big house and, like Luz, paid rent to Mrs. Mulzit. Gina's sweetheart, Luz's cousin Geraldito, was coming to pick her up from work that day. Gina wore the white dress cut low in front, with the big bow at the end of the deep V. *Stop here*, the bow seemed to say. *Stop here before it's too late*. But Geraldito never stopped at the bow, which is why Gina had a smile on her red lips as she dressed, his face smiling back in her mind. She had two hundred planters in her apartment, plastic and ceramic deer and boys pushing little carts and geese with holes in their backs for the dirt and plants. She dusted them on Saturdays, sweat moistening her upper lip.

Mrs. Mulzit sharpened her cleaver that morning, the one she kept by the front door in case of strangers. Long dead Johanni, whom she always called *my loving husband*, sold all the guns when he grew sick so they would be gone when he was. "No woman's hands on my guns," he said to her when she failed to keep the surprise from her face. He died at the kitchen table while waiting for Teresa to serve his lunch. She had gone out of the room for just a moment. Oh! If she had stayed. When she returned he was dead, slumped back in his chair, his mouth open but soundless. What was it saying to God, Teresa wondered, the open mouth? What was Johanni saying to God in his moment of judgment? That was five years ago, and every day since she has thought, had I been there when the last moment came I might have known. Now only the walls of the kitchen know.

But Johanni was gone and the cleaver leaned there by the door, and it was a good thing, too, because once she had to swing it at a white boy in overbig untied shoes who came in the unlocked door and took things up in his arms. "Who are you, you fresh boy!" she had shouted, and it had been a rare cold day, so their breath puffed out white between them while they stood there in the cold hall, each shocked by the other. Then Mrs. Mulzit ran forward and swung the cleaver. No matter that she had swung the wrong dull side at him—he leaped back and dashed out of the house. "You come back and I carve your head for you!" she screamed. Once outside, he snarled, "Old bitch, come and get me!" She slammed the door. Still outside, the boy said, "Come on, come out and get me! Get me, huh? Come on!"

She was not afraid, not anymore. Not when she saw Ed Thorns pull into the driveway and park by Gina's car in the back by the low grapevine Johanni had planted. Not when she saw Gina look out her kitchen window at the car and fluff her hair when she saw it was a man. Not even when Mrs. Mulzit saw Luz lift herself from her garden of roses, always a little dusty but pretty anyway. *Luz has a garden full of roses* was a good thing to think and to say. Luz looked toward the man without greeting him, like a mild cow, Mrs. Mulzit thought. Luz was big in the body from her ten children, all grown or nearly, who came and went like busy shoppers to her house on the weekends.

Ed Thorns surveyed the back of the house, not quite so menacing from the rear, like a heavy woman bending over. The freeways were in their high morning rush hour roar. God, it's noisy as hell, he thought, a perfect place for a car dealership, what with the advertisements for movement and speed roaring around you all the time. He saw the little grapevine, twisting lovingly around its low trellis. Amazing that anything could grow here at all, he thought. This square mile must be under a constant smog alert.

He ignored the back door yawning open and walked up the drive to the front door. Truly, it was a fine old house: three floors, the roof pitched so steep its wedges looked like blades. There was even a spire. Someone spared little expense in the last century; there were crystal doorknobs, heavy mahogany, a stained glass panel over the front doorway. The bell still worked—it looked like the original ringer. Ed thought of creamy-skinned women in velvet dresses brushing the floor, low voices, men with lush satin hats. No one wore hats anymore, or if they did, they were boys and wore cheap plastic logo caps turned insolently backwards. Ed thought you could tell the grace of the age by its popular headwear. These days, he thought, it was a dark time for grace.

He was all the more convinced of this when the door opened and a tiny, savagely thin old woman stood there, a worn apron pressing back her long breasts, a huge meat cleaver weighing down one hand.

"*Ja,*" she said. "What you want."

"Well, ma'am, I've come to see you about your house. It's Mrs. Mulzit, isn't it?"

"My house is fine."

"Yes, it is! It certainly is fine! No question about that. We love this house, yes, we do. In fact, the city loves this house so much they want to buy it and all the rest of your property. For a lot of money."

She lowered the cleaver. "Who are you?"

Ed held out his hand and wondered for a second if he would get it back. "Mrs. Mulzit, I'm Ed Thorns. From the Los Angeles Historical Society. I'm a neighborhood man myself. Used to live around here." Which wasn't true, but Ed had done so much work for the Society in this area that he might as well have lived there.

But he was a neighborhood man at home, anyway. He and his wife belonged to the neighborhood association and worked to establish a Crimewatch network. Fortunately, they didn't get too much crime up in his wealthy suburban town, but there were regular burglaries. Somebody wanted to build a big low-income housing project on the edge of town, a move that everyone feared would drive up the crime in no time. Ed and his wife, Marjorie, were going to join the group protesting this project at the city planning meeting next week.

Mrs. Mulzit put her hand in the man's and let him shake it. Her whole body shook with this brave shake. "This house is a historical treasure, ma'am, did you know that?" he said.

"*Ja*, sure, I been in this house years longer than you were born," she said. She still wasn't too sure about this young monkey. He smelled of costly department stores, and his face looked damp, as though he had bathed too long.

Ed laughed. "No doubt. May I come in?"

"Well, all right. But you take anything and I get you with this." She shook the cleaver, which, like Ed's vigorous handshake, moved her whole body. Ed knew he could pluck the cleaver out of her hand in a heartbeat, but there was a palpable, prickly energy about her. She led him through the hallway to the parlor and pointed to a plastic-covered plush chair with doilies taped over each arm. He went to it and sat. There were smiling pictures of young people all over the walls, no doubt grandchildren. A pair of paper plates stuck with dried macaroni and sprayed with gold paint were mounted like rare china over the fireplace. She sat on a footstool in front of him.

"So what you want now," she said. She folded her meaty hands.

"Your grandchildren?" he said, pointing to the walls.

"*Ja*. They all live far away. But that's none your business. So what about this house and the money. What about that?"

"Well, we'd like to buy this house and your lot for a million dollars."

Mrs. Mulzit threw back her hands as though she were in pain. "Oh, my God! So much money!" That she could have so much money seemed an affliction to her at that moment, a crisis she must act on immediately. "What then?"

"Well, we move this nice house somewhere else and make it a nice office building, and then some builders put in a big car lot here and sell cars." Ed resolved to be patient, yes, patient and gentle. He could tell the old lady was a foreigner, probably an immigrant from Germany, judging from her accent, one of the many who came to America and made it what it was. He knew his great-great grand-somebody came over from England in the last century and started the line of people who were to become him, and that was a wonder, the toughness of foreign people like them. She deserved his respect. "And you can live somewhere better, and not have to hear the cars all the time."

"So much money. How you move a whole house? Such a thing, to move a whole house."

"They lift it up with jacks, put wheels under it, and tow it away."

Mrs. Mulzit thought about that, a house on wheels, going who knows where, somewhere, leaving her behind, taking with it the image of her loving Johanni lying back dead in his chair, waiting for his lunch. He had left her that day, gone to his judgment—she had prayed, God, be merciful. There were other images, too, as real as if they hung on the walls in frames: her boy, her son with Johanni, whose height she measured by the rosewood panel half way up the hallway wall. She remembered way back, the times Johanni was drunk and hit her with things, never his hand. Back then it seemed all right, it was the thing that hit her, the thing that was to blame for getting between them.

And somewhere in that time was the thing she didn't think of much, but it was there: the man, the Swedish boy a little younger than she, who boarded in one of the extra upstairs rooms. He took her up in his arms one day, when Johanni was off fishing at the pier and her boy in school, and kissed her. She was so surprised she didn't say a word and neither did he, and they never spoke of it, though Johanni said one day weeks later, "I don't like that guy." And then the boy was gone. And all the rest of it was gone, too, except her and the house that held the things she remembered tight in its silent wood.

Ed Thoms's face: a pale round shape and nothing more. It was the heaviness of the house's wood that troubled her most. Wood does not go to God; it crumbles to ash. Johanni always said, even the day before he died, don't lose this house. But he hadn't known the days would be this long now, how dark it was inside things. How she would wake some days and not know what year it was anymore—everything looked the same. He would never have understood anyway, him. Just like a man, he didn't have enough sense to be afraid. He did not pray; she prayed for him. He did not remember; she and the house remembered for him.

"Excuse me, ma'am?" The young dandy man before her, yes— Ed Thorns. Frowning, looking puzzled.

"*Ja*, okay. I got to sign something, huh? You got something for me to sign?"

Ed couldn't believe it would be this easy. He'd expected more resistance when he'd seen that cleaver. A woman with a cleaver seemed like someone who'd have to take a big nugget of information like this away for a while, turning it over and over. "Ah, no—we just thought I'd approach you now and handle the papers later. But I can have them in the mail to you. Are you sure there's no one you want to talk to about it? Your children?"

"I can sign okay. This is a big favor for him. My son. He won't have to monkey with this big house when I die. You guys help me go somewhere else?"

"Yes, of course, the real estate company has agreed to find you another residence, wherever you want."

"How soon do I get the money?" Mrs. Mulzit felt a great hurry. She might get killed tomorrow and not have the new money, fresh in her hands like light. There was danger everywhere. One of Luz's nephews got killed by gangs just last week. Mrs. Mulzit thought, maybe they would come for Luz's landlady herself, though she dressed poor so they would think she had nothing.

Ed Thorns laughed, embarrassed. He hadn't thought little old immigrant ladies would be so greedy. "Well, there's a rather complicated procedure for the sale of historical property, but if you're in a hurry, maybe a couple of weeks. Or we can advance you some money after you sign the papers."

"Okay, then. I wait for the mail." She stood up. Ed stood up, too, feeling strange. Events had gone just the way he'd wanted them too, and somehow he was a little sorry. Or guilty, or something. The whole affair seemed wrong somehow. Mrs. Mulzit's bluish, filmy eyes stared wide past him, as though seeing busy invisible things. He left and drove to the Historical Society and gave his report, and then went home for the night. The next week he and Marjorie went to the city planning meeting, during which thoughts of Mrs. Mulzit bumped around his mind like old dreams.

Mrs. Mulzit knew that the sale of the property meant Luz and Gina would have to leave. By the time the man left, Gina had gone to work, so Mrs. Mulzit didn't have to answer any of her questions. Luz was easier, because she wouldn't ask questions. She would just make statements, and then wait for you to talk. If you didn't want to talk, you didn't have to. You just answered with one or two words, or a sentence, and Luz would know, and be quiet. Johanni hadn't wanted to rent to her and her husband. He didn't want Mexicans all over the place; they were dirty and cut each other up with knives, he said. But Mrs. Mulzit felt something wise and steady in Luz, though what it was she could not name. She's quiet, Teresa said to Johanni. Look how sad her face is, Teresa said. Like the Virgin Mary. Johanni relented, and Luz had rented from her for seventeen years, raised her many children and buried her husband. She gave Mrs. Mulzit roses from the garden. She went to Johanni's funeral. They helped each other clean the houses twice a year.

Luz came out to beat a rug when Mrs. Mulzit went down the driveway, carrying her best purse, to the garage. The two women exchanged glances, but neither spoke. Luz had been saving the rug-beating task for just this moment, and when Mrs. Mulzit didn't speak, Luz knew her premonition of the night before wasn't just women's complaints. "I knew it," she said to the clean rug, laying it back down on the dining room floor. "Something is going on here. And I don't think it is going to be good." She began scrubbing the stove, deciding to clean out the inside with the smelly oven-cleaner, since she hadn't done that for a while. The can read: *Fumes can be dangerous.*

Mrs. Mulzit drove her old Impala to the bank, the big bank with the high ceiling that swallowed everyone's voices and made them loud at the same time. Like a church. She leaned way in to the Black man at the teller's station and said in a whisper, "I want to talk to somebody about a lot of money. I want to talk private." Another man came out, this time a white man, and he took her over to a glass-enclosed office with no roof. He sat her down and gave her a cup of coffee she hadn't asked for, and listened to her tell about the house and all the money. "I want something lighter than a big house. Do you know what I am saying? I am not so big no more."

"Well, ma'am, there is gold."

Gold. Johanni had told her once, from watching some show on the television, that gold never rusts, never ages, always lasts even if thrown away. Some museum somewhere had gold from a couple thousand years ago, when Jesus was alive, and it was as shiny and new as the day they made it. Women in India put gold jewelry all over their bodies when they got married, showing their worth to all assembled. The show said, gold would last at the bottom of the sea forever.

The man told her about dollars per ounce and gold bars and safes and Switzerland and Africa. It became so clear, like the sun coming up over the eastern buildings on a clear day: this is what she would leave her family, something that would be perfect forever, even if they went ahead and sold it. That would be okay with her, as long as what they got from her was nice and shiny and had clean edges and stacked well. It seemed her whole life had been spent washing and cleaning and dusting and fighting against things getting messy and dirty and wearing out. It was so simple she thought herself a silly woman for not thinking of it before. She was so happy. She went home with brochures and his business card, and encouragement to come again when she was ready to spend her money.

It was a bright, bright day outside, and Mrs. Mulzit was still happy when she went out to her car and got in to go home. But she didn't want to drive right back to the big house and to Luz out in the garden. At the thought of going home, she felt ashamed, though when she ticked off her actions, the way she did on her rosary when she was a little girl in Austria, she couldn't think of anything she had done wrong. She knew that sometimes God sends you shame in advance, so you don't do something shameful later. She would have to be careful.

She went to the food store and bought a nice coffee cake, a gooey one with raspberry jelly oozing out under the icing. Smiling children's faces looked out at her from the package wrap. It would be all right. She would go home and put the jelly cake between her and Luz, and then Gina would come home and join them, and they would coo at the luscious cake and pat their hips and thighs, as if to keep the pounds from settling there. And then she would say to them, so now, this house is going away, as though it was doing so of its own will, like a child leaving home. They would say Oh! and Gina would say, *I've been wanting a new apartment, closer to Geraldito*, and Luz would say, *Yes, it is time for a place with more roses*. And the late daylight as they sat there would be so pretty, through the old lace curtains, on the three of them together. It would seem right that they all go off, away from the house and its invisible pictures on the walls.

But that wasn't at all how it went. When Luz saw the jelly cake, held up for her to see by Mrs. Mulzit as she made her way from the car to the house, Luz said, "What did I do?"

"What you talking, what did I do? I want that you come have a little cake with me. That's all."

"I have not done anything for you to evict me," Luz said, standing up straight. She imagined all her children behind her, as when they were small, peeping around her fearfully.

Mrs. Mulzit glared at Luz, furious that Luz should be so fresh. With her fierce face and the graying hair in her black braid, Luz suddenly looked to Mrs. Mulzit like one of the women following Jesus in her picture Bible. One of the ones who won Jesus' love even though she had sinned and had many husbands.

"You're a crazy woman," Mrs. Mulzit said, curling her body around her package of cake and turning her back on Luz. "You go think those crazy things by yourself." She went into the house and let the door bang behind her. A car drove in the back yard—it was Gina, with Geraldito, home for lunch. The noon sun was stark and ugly on the ground. Gina's car: a cheap foreign job. But then she saw Gina and Geraldito go to Luz and begin talking with her, and then Luz pointing at the big house. Mrs. Mulzit shrank away from the window. Soon there was a knock on the back door.

Gina was there. "You evicting Luz?" Geraldito looked on from the bottom step, his hair a slick wave across his head. He was too handsome for his own good.

"No, Jesu Maria, NO!" Mrs. Mulzit shouted. "It's the house that's going!" Now Gina was fresh, always had been, like all Italians. Sometimes you had to shout at her. But she was so girlish and pretty in her white dress, Mrs. Mulzit felt ashamed at her own orange-pink print housecoat, smudged at the hips where her hands kept going.

"You selling the house? You don't got to evict Luz for that," Gina said. Geraldito nodded, just behind her. "She's been there a long time," he added.

"No—*dammte*, I mean yes. I sell the house, *ja*. But the men going to take the house away, too. Not just us. I'm too old to run this place no more. There are cars coming. They are going to park cars here. We have to get out of the way. Don't you hear them?" Mrs. Mulzit put up her hand to quiet the wordless Gina and Geraldito, to stop them from staring at her with their mouths open. The noon traffic sounded like a fire roaring, or flood water rising from a deep ravine. It seemed louder than it ever had.

"Missus, you said us? You mean me, too?" Gina did not want to be a baby, but she could not stop the tears from filling up her eyes. All her little planters with the bits of green growing in them, arranged just right—

"Mrs. Mulzit, you can't move a whole house. Are you all okay, *señora?*" Geraldito said.

Luz had appeared behind them. "So it is true," she said, after listening. "Okay, then. I will find somewhere else to go now. I came here from México. I will go to somewhere else from here. I know how to do that. You do what you know how to do, yes?" She stepped up onto the wide step beside Gina, her long face nearing Mrs. Mulzit's. "I just want to know, lady, do you know how to go somewhere else from this house? Do you know how to watch it go away from here?"

"I know how to do things just fine," Mrs. Mulzit snapped. "Never you mind about me."

"Well, then, God be with you, Mrs. Mulzit," Luz said, turning back toward her house.

"Yes, that's right," Geraldito said, taking Gina by the hand. "God bless you, Mrs. Mulzit. God bless you." And then they went away too, toward Gina's apartment across the courtyard, one flight up.

Mrs. Mulzit had a mouth full of heat. She went to the sink and spat into it. "Those *dammte* women," she said. "And that Geraldito, with his shiny hair—" She felt her face purse up, as though she were tasting lemons, and she spat again. A cry came out of her, a wail like a birthing woman, but she wouldn't have tears—no. Her cry sounded up to the ceiling of the kitchen and up the stairs to the bedrooms and the bath, everywhere.

It was much like the long wooden screams and groans from the beams and joists and floorboards of the great house itself, as the workmen jacked up its corners from the ground several weeks later, after Luz's whole family came and moved all her things from her house into small trucks and cars and taken them and her away. Gina had long since moved in with Geraldito. Both Gina's and Luz's small buildings fell under the bulldozer, their splintered fragments hauled away. Mrs. Mulzit held a cat that had come from nowhere while movers put her things into yellow vans and drove them miles away into the suburbs, to her tiny new house with gold carpet and hard sun in the windows every morning.

The great house shivered when the workmen at last removed the jacks and let its full weight down on the net of wheeled steel girders they had thrust beneath it. It was so tall that Ed Thorns had to call the city utilities manager and arrange for a power crew to lower the lines the day of the move. But all Ed could get was three hours—from three to six a.m. Working madly in the orange streetlight half-dark, the crew unhooked each block of lines to let the house pass and then hooked them up again. By five-thirty they had made it as far as Adams Boulevard, where cars began to pour down from the Harbor Freeway. They were a mile from the old site with yet a mile to go to the new. There was no choice. They left the house on its wheeled girders in the middle of Figueroa, until predawn of the next day would empty the streets again.

All day, children pointed at the house and screamed for their friends. Adults stopped to gawk. Photojournalists took pictures for their newspapers. And, as it happened, Mrs. Mulzit and Gina and Luz all went by the house that day as it sat there on its wheels. Luz was taking a walk; her new apartment was not far away from the old. Gina was driving to work. And Mrs. Mulzit had driven back to West 18th Street, though she didn't know why. There was nothing at her old address anymore: just damp, turned-up ground. Wood trash.

But when she turned down Figueroa and saw the house towering there, attached to nothing, cars flowing around it, she thought, and would always think, how tall and grand a house it was. How far it was to her new house. How anything can be moved.

Acknowledgments

Thanks to the following journals & magazines in which these stories originally appeared:

"Bad," *North American Review* (Summer 2002)

"The Visitor," *The Sun* (January 1996)

"Vaguely Spanish," *Denver Quarterly* (Summer 2000)

"Florida Postcards," *Willow Springs* (1997)

"The Door in the Woods," *Daedalus* (Summer 2006)

"Camarado," *Other Voices* (Spring/Summer 2003)

"Vacation," *Ascent* (Fall 1995)

"We Keep No Animals," *Seattle Review* (1997)

"The Physics of Suspension," *The Sun* (November 1997)

"Flight," *Hopewell Review* (Fall 1996)

"The House on Figueroa," *Beloit Fiction Journal* (Spring 1994)

The following stories were collected into *Household Lies* (Winnow Press: 2005): "Bad," "Vaguely Spanish," "The Visitor," "Flight," "The House on Figueroa," "We Keep No Animals," "The Physics of Suspension," "Camarado," "Florida Postcards."

Dorian Gossy's short fiction & and essays have appeared in the following magazines: North American Review, The Sun, Seattle Review, Other Voices, Beloit Fiction Journal, Daedalus, Willow Springs, and others. She has taught creative writing in university, elementary school, local art center, & federal prison settings. She is a licensed clinical social worker and lives in the Adirondack Mountains of New York with her husband, the poet Roger Mitchell.

www.ingramcontent.com/pod-product-compliance
Lightning Source LLC
Chambersburg PA
CBHW030531020726
47494CB00004B/1307